GUIDEPOSTS

CHURCH CHOIR
MYSTERIES™

Mischief in Mason City

Evelyn Minshull

Guideposts®

CARMEL, NEW YORK 10512

www.guidepostsbooks.com

www.guidepostsbooks.com
Guideposts Books & Inspirational Media Division
Series Editor: Michele Slung
Cover art by Stephen Gardner & Edgar Jerins
Cover design by Wendy Bass
Interior design by José R. Fonfrias
Interior cat illustrations by Viqui Maggio
Typeset by Composition Technologies, Inc.
Printed in the United States of America

Richard and Grace Anna Boggs,
whose Mercer Mercantile Ice Cream and Soda Shoppe
preserves the flavor of the late 1800s,
including an ornate tin ceiling . . .

and Grace Wagner,
who will recognize the reason.

Acknowledgments

WHAT FUN—and what a privilege, as well—to be a writer involved in the inspiring shenanigans of Gracie and her Willow Bend cohorts! My heartfelt thanks go to editors Elizabeth Kramer Gold, commander-in-chief; Michele Slung, who keeps us consistent; and Stephanie Castillo Samoy, who makes us look good. And, of course, to the other authors involved in the "Church Choir Mysteries" series. It's a treat to receive each new book!

1

"OF COURSE YOU'LL GO." Uncle Miltie, hands dripping suds, turned from the sink. He looked indignantly at Gracie Parks, his niece. "How could you say no to that sweet little Lacey Carpenter?"

Gracie Lynn Parks hesitated. Much as she admired Gillian Pomeroy—Lacey's flamboyant grandmother—and yearned to involve herself in her most recent assault on "progress," and much as she loved catering weddings, there were other considerations.

Uncle Miltie, for one. Gracie hated leaving him alone. A spry octogenarian, George Morgan—whose nickname stemmed from his weakness for corny jokes, in the style of a long-ago TV comedian—had lived with her in her comfortable clapboard house in Willow Bend, Indiana, since the death of his wife.

"I can take care of myself, you know." He was back

at work, clinking silverware against china. "Done it before," he continued. "Nobody nursemaided me through World War II."

She didn't remind him that he had been a lot younger then, and simply smiled at the thought.

When it came right down to it, she understood that her reluctance went beyond concern for Uncle Miltie and Gooseberry, the large orange cat who controlled both their schedules. The truth was, she had to admit, she hated leaving Willow Bend itself.

Plus, there was her beloved Eternal Hope Community Church. Only for her annual holiday with her late husband Elmo, and for visits to her son Arlen's family in New York, had she ever missed two consecutive Sundays there.

"It isn't that far—" she began.

Uncle Miltie cut her short. "Don't even think of scurrying from there to here and back again, like some demented wind-up toy. You'll only exhaust yourself." He chuckled.

"Even without you, Barb will still manage to keep Estelle from shattering the window glass with her high C." He was speaking of the Eternal Hope choir director and one of their more ambitious singers. "And Pastor Paul, too, can manage without you, whatever you might believe. That young fellow's really coming along."

They both adored their boyish minister and had watched

him steadily grow in the job, becoming stronger and wiser in his pastoral mission.

Gracie sighed. "Oh, Uncle Miltie, I just don't know—"

As if on cue, the telephone rang, startling them for an instant.

"I'll get it." Uncle Miltie moved slowly but steadily toward the shrill sound on his arthritis-impaired legs. He was proud of his ability to propel himself around, often through sheer willpower on bad days, and often with the help of a walker or double canes. Today, though, was one of the good ones, and Gracie watched with affection as he spoke on the phone. He was a tough old bird—she just couldn't help worrying about him.

"That settles it, then." He replaced the receiver with a loud clink.

She had heard the murmur of his reassuring tones but had no idea what the conversation was about. She had been lost in her thoughts about the wedding supper she might make if she took Gillian Pomeroy up on her invitation.

"That was Clint Whitley, an old Army buddy in Pittsburgh. He needs someone to stay with him after an operation. I said I'd come. I can go on the bus. I do believe you're fresh out of excuses, my dear!" Uncle Miltie looked excited.

"Fresh out of excuses!" he repeated.

WOULDN'T YOU REALLY RATHER FLY?" Marge Lawrence, Gracie's neighbor and best friend, paused with a steaming mug of tea held to her lips. Her multicolored rings and bracelets glittered in the bright morning light pouring in Gracie's kitchen windows.

Uncle Miltie pursed his lips. "Fly? Why yes, I'd love to, Marge—if God had thought to give me wings."

"He didn't equip you with wheels, either," Gracie commented dryly. "So why isn't the bus out, too?"

Uncle Miltie snorted. "Good one, Gracie!"

Marge rolled her eyes. These friends loved to tease each other but, truth be told, Uncle Miltie hated to be gotten the best of. If the punchlines weren't his own, he tended not to hear them. This time, however, he'd been had, fair and square.

"Know why birds have wing feathers instead of porcupine quills?" He smiled in happy anticipation. The ball was back in his court and he was preparing a slam.

Though Marge grumbled about Uncle Miltie's fondness for riddles, she knew better than to try and resist. "The quills would point them in the wrong direction?"

"You can do better than that!"

Gracie, for her part, was willing to listen patiently, though frequently she, too, tried her hand at being her uncle's straight man.

Marge sighed. Then she guessed again. "The quills would cut short their chirping?"

"*Hmmph.*"

"Okay, then they'd poke holes in the clouds, and we'd have nonstop rain. And that's all I'm going to say!" She glared a challenge.

"All right, I'll help you out of your misery. But you really should have been able to do better, Marge, my girl. The answer's quite simple."

Uncle Miltie tipped himself back in his chair. "If they were on birds, then they'd be called *bird* quills—not *porcupine* quills."

"George Morgan—" sputtered Marge. "You are the most infuriating man in the state of Indiana."

"I'd hoped for this side the Mississippi," he said smugly.

Dear Lord.... Gracie was in full prayer-walk mode, wearing her headphones and swinging along as though she were at least a decade younger than her sixty-something years. She felt both energized and uplifted.

There was, however, a slight panic brought on by all she needed to get done—and yet here was the grace of Michael Faircloth's nimble fingers on the piano keyboard. She listened contentedly.

Gracie often played CDs as she walked. Many mornings, Gaither choruses or the crystal phrasings of Charlotte Church echoed her soul's needs and joys. But just as often, she preferred instrumental background to her thoughts. This was one of those occasions.

Lord, how will I ever get Uncle Miltie ready in time? And the house? Will Marge drown the potted plants again—or manage to create a desert, like the one on her own kitchen windowsill? Will she remember to sprinkle the garden rows with ammonia water? Those tender little seedlings are such a temptation for rabbits....

Gooseberry darted ahead, then turned to wait so he could once again twine himself around her ankles. He was her accustomed morning companion, but from time to time their interpretations of the proper pace differed.

"Sorry." She bent to pet him before resuming her conversation with God. *This invitation to Mason City may be Your way of stirring me up a bit. It's just the getting ready that I mind, since I'm sure the actual going will be fine.*

She could admit only to herself that she worried about Uncle Miltie's going off all by himself for the first time since he'd come to live with her. It felt a little like the first day she'd watched Arlen run toward the schoolyard while she waited by the curb. He had been fine, of course; kids usually were. But it hadn't diminished her young mother's sense of apprehension for months—no, years—to come.

Uncle Miltie, of course, was more than seven decades past the playgrounds of his youth. Still, he was her charge, just as Arlen had been, and sometimes he was just as much of a little boy, despite his gray hairs.

Gracie quickened her pace, and Gooseberry scurried to keep up. She thought back to how this visit to Mason City had first been set into motion.

The call had come on a lazy Sunday afternoon as Gracie relaxed with a crossword puzzle and Uncle Miltie and Rocky Gravino played a heated game of Scrabble.

"You'd think," Uncle Miltie berated his opponent, "any newspaper editor worth his printer's ink would recognize a perfectly legitimate word like *committable*!"

"Then why can't we find it in the dictionary?"

"Even Webster didn't know everything!"

"No," chuckled the publisher of the *Mason County Gazette*. "Then how come it isn't *Morgan's Dictionary*?"

Mercifully, the phone rang.

"Mrs. Parks?" a sweet, high-pitched young voice asked. "Mrs. Parks, are you there?"

"Lacey!"

"You remember my voice!" The child laughed with delight.

"Of course I do!" Not long ago, Lacey Carpenter had been a visitor to Willow Bend and quickly carved out a special spot in Gracie's affection. "How's your grandmother? And your aunt?"

Lacey giggled. "Gram's as happy as a pig in mud. That's what she tells Deke, who's going to be my new dad, sort of. Aunt Kelly's pretty happy, too. And you're doing the food—at least we hope you are, because you're the best. Everyone says so."

This was a lot of exciting news to take in, but wasn't Lacey going to stop to take a breath?

Apparently not.

"And besides, Gram needs you 'cause there's mysterious stuff happening here, and Gram says nobody's better than Gracie Parks at detective work. That means you!"

Gracie laughed but still listened carefully. Was this simply a matter of a child's overactive imagination, or was something troubling really going on in Mason City, where she and Gillian lived?

"Most of it's funny, really," Lacey continued. "Mrs. McQuaid sputtered a lot when her rose garden fence was painted with giant Japanese beetles. She went right out and spray-painted over them. But you can still see the shapes, if you look really hard. And it's honestly kind of sad, because those beetles looked *real*, except a thousand times too big. I'd never realized how beautiful Japanese beetles are. Have you?"

Gracie wasn't certain she was meant to answer.

"But the mall part *is* scary," Lacey went on. Now her tone was more sober. "Gram gets phone calls all the time. Really nasty ones!" She gave a sigh.

"But, gosh, you wouldn't believe how excited I am about the wedding! I'm going to wear a beautiful dress! Deke's a really good guy. And you *will* do the rehearsal dinner, won't you? And the wedding reception? Oh, I can't wait until you see my dress! It's lacy, just like me! And I'm singing, too. 'O Perfect Love' and 'O Promise Me' and maybe a mushy song Aunt Kelly and Deke are writing together. I just hope I don't cry! But I know I will. Will you bring Gooseberry along?

"And Gram says she won't even hear of you staying less than two weeks at least! We want you—we *need* you—for that long, to hold our hand, Gram says. But we've got four hands, or maybe I mean eight, at least, so I don't see how you can hold them all at once! But you *will* come to Mason City, won't you? Pretty, pretty, *pretty* please?"

At that point Lacey paused for breath. Her grandmother, Gillian Pomeroy, was a fiery community activist, always protesting against some environmental outrage or civic injustice, and Lacey had obviously inherited some of her staying power.

Lacey's Aunt Kelly had been briefly married to Grif Ransen, a man who'd turned out to be a rather nasty piece of work. Now, obviously, she was trying the altar a second time, and Gracie could only pray that, with this choice, God would smile on dear Kelly's union as He had on her own.

"Are you coming, Mrs. Parks? Are you?" Lacey broke into her thoughts, and Gracie realized she hadn't yet replied.

"Let me think about it, my dear," Gracie told her. "I do miss your smiling face, but I also have Uncle Miltie to contend with. Let me get back to you."

3

LOOKING OUT THE KITCHEN WINDOW, Gracie thought, *Lord, isn't there something a bit dangerous, almost sinful, about the fragrance of hot cinnamon rolls? Magnets, that's what they are! Why else would people move like zombies toward a smell?*

Uncle Miltie, already under the spell of the aroma, was making his way toward the porch. And Marge, her little Shih-Tzu Charlotte beside her, seemed about to follow.

Gracie was baking a triple batch. Some were for Uncle Miltie to snack on during his long bus trip, and there was a full dozen for Marge as a thank-you for looking out for the house. The rest Gracie would take along to Mason City.

Tomorrow, Lord! Since I agreed to go, the time has sped by faster than I could get my bearings! How can I remember everything? Only with Your help, I believe, as I head off in the joyous certainty I'm acting as a watchful servant in Your name—

whether here at home in Willow Bend or over there in Mason City.

Breathing deeply of the intoxicating cinnamon perfumes, she turned as the kitchen door rattled and admitted not only Uncle Miltie and Marge but Rocky Gravino, as well.

Her newspaper editor friend lightly patted Gracie's shoulder before easing his bulk into a kitchen chair.

She turned to smile at him, teasingly. "So you sniffed out my cinnamon rolls from all the way across town?"

"That aroma should be outlawed! It makes strong men weak. But I was on my way here, anyway—and maybe I was hoping. . . ."

Gracie took the hint. She cut into the Mason City pan. What choice did she have?

"One's a good start." Uncle Miltie sampled the icing of his roll first. "A start, mind you."

Before sitting down to join her uncle and friends, Gracie opened the screen door for Gooseberry, so that he and Charlotte could scamper off on one of their mysterious animal quests.

"They don't know what they're missing," Marge proclaimed, licking her sticky fingertips. "Gracie, these are heavenly—as usual!"

"If this is what they serve in heaven," Rocky joked, "then sign me up." Gracie prudently said nothing, since she knew Rocky's pastry-loving habits were far stronger than his churchgoing ones.

"Speaking of Charlotte," Uncle Miltie said, "what do you get when you cross a fish with a Shih-Tzu?"

"I don't think we were speaking of my little angel," Marge corrected him. "But, maybe, just because she's left the room, you feel free to talk about her."

Out in the yard, Gooseberry and Charlotte were engaged in contemplation of more important things.

"Please," Uncle Miltie said impatiently. "Just answer the question."

Finally, Rocky said, "Okay, I'll bite. What *do* you get when you cross Marge's mutt with a fish?"

"You get pooched salmon," Uncle Miltie pronounced, slapping his thigh in triumph.

Nudging the car windshield with his nose, Gooseberry meowed forlornly as the bus, belching black smoke, pulled away from the curb.

"I know, dear." Gracie rubbed the soft spot behind his ears. "We'll miss him, won't we? But not for long. We're embarking on an adventure of our own!"

Gooseberry gave her a suspicious look, then settled back into the passenger seat in apparent resignation. Fannie Mae, Gracie's venerable dark blue Cadillac, was packed as if Gracie were headed to Alaska, not a nearby town. But a soft, faded pillow was all that adorned the front seat, aside from Gooseberry's pumpkin-colored bulk.

On her way out of town, Gracie decided to stop for a minute at the church office. There she found Pastor Paul with Mandy Crispen, president of the Youth Fellowship. Mandy—fresh-faced, ponytailed and jean-clad—fairly exuded adoration, a fact to which Pastor Paul thankfully seemed oblivious.

And it's a good thing, too, Lord—for how could he possibly shepherd Your Eternal Hope sheep if he knew how many of them—and not just teenagers—were targeting him for their romantic aspirations?

"Gracie!" Paul shoved back his chair and hurried over. He gave her a warm hug in greeting. "And so you're leaving us for how long? Two whole weeks? How will we manage?"

Gracie laughed. "Not so well, I hope, that you realize you don't need me at all! But I did want to drop in and say good-bye!"

"I'm delighted you did." He smiled at Mandy. "Let Gracie be an example to you. She's as wise and kind as she is generous and loving. And she's a splendid cook, to boot! What more could I ask from a devoted parishioner?"

Gracie noticed Mandy's scowl, but also saw that Paul failed to.

Gracie touched the girl's arm. "Mandy dear, you look like you're on your way out. Will you walk with me to the parking lot?"

"Sure, Mrs. Parks." Under her breath she muttered, "Maybe some of your perfection will rub off on me."

Pastor Paul, already busy in his office, couldn't possibly have heard.

"He thinks I'm only a kid." Mandy kicked a stone from the path as they left the building. When Gracie didn't respond at once, she added, "But I'm not." She looked up fiercely. "I know what you're thinking, Mrs. Parks. Mom says it all the time."

Gracie patted the girl's slender shoulder. "I'm only thinking that you're a lovely young woman and that Pastor Paul is lucky to have you as someone who admires him. But we all do, just remember that—he means as much to all of us."

Mandy watched Gracie open her car door. "Well, don't you think the Lord would rather I have a crush on a minister, a true servant of His, than, say, a football player?"

Gracie laughed. "You're also a very bright young woman, and I'll be happy to debate you when I get back from Mason City. Don't think I don't remember having romantic fantasies about unsuitable people when I was your age! I got over them, and so will you. In the meantime, keep in mind your commitment to Eternal Hope—the youth group needs as much of your attention and energy as you have to spare. You've been doing a splendid job!"

"Thanks, Mrs. Parks! I needed to hear that." Mandy managed a smile.

Glancing at the clock, Gracie realized that, to keep to the schedule she'd set for herself, there wasn't going to be time to say good-bye to everyone as she'd planned. She took a deep breath and consciously pushed away any sense of guilt. After all, it wasn't as if she were deserting anyone. They'd, every one of them, encouraged her to go.

Abe's Deli, then, would be her next and final stop. She'd be able to combine lunch and conversation, and—if owner Abe Wasserman was in one of his more philosophical moods—she'd depart with an extra dose of useful wisdom, as well.

As it turned out, her friend Abe did not disappoint in cuisine or companionship. And an added bonus was Rocky Gravino's unexpected appearance.

"Late lunch," he said. "There was a breaking story at the Willow Mart. Seems a tarantula hitched a ride on a bunch of bananas. They rushed the stock boy who found it over to the emergency room." He grinned. "It seems he'll recover."

Abe's eyes widened. "He's a lucky kid! Tarantula bites are pretty serious, I thought."

Rocky shook his head. "Sheer fright, that's all he was suffering from. The spider was thoroughly dead. And, believe me, no one was attempting CPR!"

"Did I ever tell you about—" Abe broke off at Rocky's chuckle. "Ah, but you know my tale before I have even begun with 'A long time ago. . . .'"

"If it's about Robert Bruce, yes. It's one I remember from school, and just about the only spider story I know, except for Little Miss Muffett."

"Robert Bruce was the Scottish leader who was inspired by a spider to try one more time and so achieve victory."

"That very one," Rocky agreed.

"And what," asked Abe, smiling broadly, "what, I ask you, might a mere cook and bottle-washer like myself have in common with such a warrior?"

"Courage," Gracie suggested. "Dedication. Determination."

"You mean the courage to try sister Sophie's latest culinary experiment? Dedication to such friendships as these I cherish? Determination," he said, chuckling, "to get my new spider story told before nightfall? That is, if my friend here doesn't insist on editing it for length."

Shaking his head, Rocky leaned forward expectantly, his elbows placed squarely on the red formica tabletop.

Gracie smiled. He enjoys Abe's stories as much as anyone, she realized, though he'd probably rather surrender his press card than admit it.

"A long time ago," Abe began, then waited for their familiar laughter. "A long time ago, an elderly widow lived within sight of the bright waters of the Sea of Galilee. From the hovel she called home, she watched the fishermen splay their white cotton nets against the blueness, heard their conversations and singing as they waited for the nets to fill, watched as they heaved the nets—weighted and throbbing with fish—on board. Her husband had been a fisherman. How she missed him—his companionship, his voice, his beaming smile as he presented a plate of tasty fish to her as though she were a queen."

Gracie took a heavy breath, hoping her friends wouldn't notice. *This is getting too close to home, Lord. Even after all these years, my yearning for Elmo is sometimes too fierce to bear.*

But Abe was continuing. "The woman had long since spent her savings, what little there had been. There were no children, no brothers." He smiled. "No welfare office or Health and Human Services Department. The kindness of neighbors assured that she seldom lacked flour and salt for bread. Occasionally a fish lay at her door—the gift of an older fisherman who still remembered her husband. And the small banana tree in her dooryard furnished her fruit in season, while a cluster of palms gave her shade, and hibiscus bloomed crimson against her outer wall. Still, even though the shade was a cooling comfort and she fed her soul on the beauty about her, there were times when her stomach knotted with hunger. Even more often, times when her heart cried in its loneliness.

"It was after the spring rains that the spider moved in. 'A spider!' she declared. 'Not in my clean house!' She was about to sweep it out with the dust and breadcrumbs when it scampered across the floor and up the wall to a windowsill. The woman gasped when she saw the work of art the industrious arachnid had woven across her window. Luminous filaments danced in the breeze yet retained their perfect pattern. The morning sun caught and lit tiny droplets that beaded each thread.

"'Ah,' the woman said. 'You put the finest lacemakers to shame! How can I banish you?' Instead, she invited passing children in to admire the marvelous web. Later, one child brought her a sticky cake, another offered a wilting anemone he himself had plucked from a rocky hillside. The woman put the flower in water and set it where the spider might also enjoy it.

"Each night the spider spun. Each morning, the woman awoke to a new wonder. At length, every window was latticed, forcing her to stoop to go out the doorway, and the banana tree itself was festooned with gossamer lace. The neighbors' children were enchanted. One asked, 'Will the spider eat the bananas, since no one else can get near to them?' The woman shrugged. The bananas were not quite ripe. Enough to worry about that in a week or so.

"The spider spun a slender thread to the palm trees, and in a series of nights created a vast wall of delicate design. Now, even the mothers of the children came to admire the spider's handiwork. Sometimes, they brought a measure of flour or some fresh-churned butter, and the woman made crusty bread so that she would not notice the inviting aroma of ripening bananas.

"One afternoon, to everyone's amazement, a tour bus

detoured to the small house made magnificent by the artistry of the spider.

"'Where do we pay admission?' the bus driver asked, and the woman simply stared. The driver shrugged and said, 'The woman cannot speak. Ten shekels each should be enough.' He took a jug from the ledge near the banana tree and collected their coins. What a merry noise they made as they jangled within the pottery!

"Even as the bus roared away, the woman was unable to speak. So many shekels! She could buy flour and salt for many loaves of bread! She could give to the neighbors who had given to her! She could make sweet candies for the children, perhaps even build a bigger house with many more windows for the spider to decorate! More magnificent webs would certainly translate to more visitors and more wealth!

"However, her dreaming had made her hungry, and now she went to her banana tree to extricate one of the small, golden bananas. Picking delicately with her fingertips, she tore a fragment of the spider's lace. Still, she could not quite free the banana. The rip lengthened. No problem. Her prolific spider could make another, even grander web. Without care, she snapped another filament and broke the banana from its stem. Slowly, smiling, she peeled back the yellow skin. Never—except for Eve's apple—had fruit tasted so sweet!

"The next morning, the woman awoke to find no new webwork. Nor the morning following that. Nor ever again."

Pouring a glass of ice water, Abe leaned back in his chair.

"And . . .?" prompted Rocky.

"Forgive me." Abe refilled Rocky's glass.

"Not the water." Rocky scowled. "The story."

"It's an old one," Abe said mildly.

"At least ten minutes old!"

"At least," Abe agreed equably.

Gracie smiled. How she loved these two dear friends!

Rocky prodded. "But it's not finished!"

"Oh?" Abe looked puzzled. "It isn't? What remains to be said?"

"There's no point to it! What's the reader supposed to take away?"

"What would you suggest, my friend? That the spider—distraught that her work had been destroyed—gave up her art? That the woman—corrupted by the thought of riches—was no longer worthy of such beauty? That someone coveted and stole the spider, carrying her far away to enhance other vistas? Or possibly the woman had stumbled, killing the artist with an accidental misstep? Or perhaps it is like life—where many stories are never completed, and where often there seems no point."

"I never learn, do I?" said Rocky, grinning. "But that's the point, too, I fear."

Abe raised an eyebrow. "Must all life be about learning, my friend? Isn't simply 'being' sometimes enough?"

Rocky laughed. "My only question is, what would the story have been like if that tarantula at the Willow Mart had been a live one?"

Gracie waited for Abe's reaction.

The deli owner took it in his stride. "Rocky, my friend, have a piece of pie on the house. The banana cream, I think, might be appropriate."

ALTHOUGH GRACIE HAD VISITED the Mason County courthouse hundreds of times, she still experienced a momentary sense of civic pride whenever its gold-ribbed dome appeared on the horizon. And so it was this day, even though both dome and building were practically obscured by scaffoldings.

Long ago, on a visit there, Elmo had boasted quietly, "You'd have to go a long way to find as impressive a structure!"

Gracie agreed. And then went him one better. To her, in fact, it was the most beautiful county courthouse on the face of the earth! Built of Indiana limestone in the infancy of the twentieth century, it had replaced a frame building lost to fire. Most days, pigeons perched on the ledges near the large clocks set within the dome to face the four directions of the compass.

Remembering that visit together, she smiled. Admiring its architectural beauty back when she was a young bride, she'd perhaps paid more attention to the rhythm of Elmo's heart-beats against her fingers than to the courthouse's polished marble floors or carved cornices. Holding hands, they'd wandered through it, and Gracie had so loved the history her young husband knowledgeably imparted.

However, it certainly looked different these days, caged in a web of wooden and metal supports. It made her think of Abe's spider. But this "web" clung, protecting the courthouse, not competing with it in artistry.

Thank You, Lord—that You didn't let them demolish this wonderful building and put up instead something that carried no sense of that wonderful past, that history that so deepens and enriches our sense of the present. I'll wager some of today's modern court-houses look more like shopping centers than magnificent halls of democracy, though I know, of course, Your presence is in those, too.

Shopping center. She sighed, recalling the reason for this visit. Or, at least one of the reasons.

What she had learned, in further conversations with Lacey's grandmother Gillian Pomeroy, discussing Kelly's wedding plans, was that she had spearheaded a movement to save the courthouse. Her opponents included a man named Tyrone Sanders, along with various local officials. Their position was that it was fiscally foolhardy to spend over nine million dollars to restore a structure that could be replaced for less than half that.

At this moment, however, Gillian was involved in a fight to

protect a beloved local park from the encroachment of unnecessary development.

Thank You, Lord, Gracie prayed, *for the Gillian Pomeroys of
the world. Without their staunch courage, their common sense and
their vision, there would be fewer historic landmarks standing, and
fewer clear rivers or lakes, too. Even Your glorious redwood forests
would have been reduced to toothpicks!*

She heard a meow. Gooseberry stretched on the seat beside
her.

"Nearly there!" she reassured him. "Even you'll admit this
is a short trip."

He made no comment. A veteran traveler when it came to
long walks, he would always prefer his own locomotion to
that of Fannie Mae's.

"You'll like seeing Lacey again, won't you?"

His loud breathing indicated that he might have again
opted for the kind of fast nap his species was known for.

Stopping for a red light, Gracie allowed herself a long look
back at the courthouse. Workers, miniaturized at this distance,
crawled on the scaffolding. Three of them stooped near the
gaping socket where a clock would eventually be reinserted.

Since barricades and yellow tape closed off South Diamond
Street, Gracie was about to take the next left when she braked
suddenly, jolting Gooseberry awake and triggering the
screeching of tires behind her.

Surely she couldn't have seen what she thought she saw!

Signaling belatedly, she slid into the first empty parking slot. The driver following her was unforgiving, and blasted his horn angrily as he roared past.

Gooseberry made a protesting noise, clambering under the steering wheel and onto Gracie's lap.

"No, truly," she soothed, "I deserved it. But I thought I saw—"

Rubbing Gooseberry's head, she rechecked the landscape she'd just passed. There, near the bandstand and the monuments to various wars stood, as always, the statue of Gen. Alistair Mason, who had given the city and county his name.

Only one thing had changed. His gallant steed had been transformed by a paintbrush into an Appaloosa—the rump of General Mason's mount now decorated lavishly with clusters of red, white and blue stars that echoed the spattered markings of that American breed of riding horse.

Gracie had barely adjusted to the cosmetic adjustments to the statue when a chanting band of picketers suddenly rounded the corner. Easing Gooseberry carefully from her lap, she opened the car door and moved toward the action.

Even before she saw the tall woman with unruly gray hair at the front of the protest group, she knew Gillian Pomeroy would be visible somewhere. After all, this was her home turf.

SAVE DOGWOOD PARK!

WHO SAYS PROGRESS MAKES PERFECT?

PARKS! NOT PERKS!

"Gracie!" Gillian Pomeroy's face broke into a wide smile. Excusing herself from the determined band she was leading, she caught the visitor from Willow Bend in a gigantic hug. Tugging Gracie back to the chanting group, she commandeered another picket sign to place in Gracie's hand.

Much as Gracie admired and respected Gillian, as she'd just told the Lord, she didn't feel entirely at home in this milling—and militant—gathering. Briefly, she struggled against the determined swell of marchers. They weren't many, but they surely were motivated.

Gooseberry, her very own independent thinker waiting in the car, would no doubt approve. So would Marge, who had a bit of the activist in her own genetic code. Rocky would simply shake his head and let that maddening twinkle light his eyes. And Pastor Paul? She felt a fond twinge for this earnest and dedicated young man. For Pastor Paul, the spectacle would undoubtedly be the raw material for a sermon, but then most things were.

Gracie did her best to blend in, although it was a difficult task for someone with such raspberry-colored curls.

"March like you mean it, dearie!" someone prodded her from behind. Gracie had little choice but to step up her pace.

Peering at her own sign, she saw that it read: DOGWOOD PARK OR DESIGNER JEANS?

Well, Lord, that's easy enough, isn't it? Remembering Arlen's joyful afternoons in the park at Willow Bend, she raised her picket sign high and joined in.

"Save Dogwood Park for the children!" she shouted. It was amazing how easy it was. Especially when it came from the heart.

Soon the air positively reverberated with Gracie's call to arms. "Save Dogwood Park for the children! Save Dogwood Park for the children!" Bystanders began applauding and whistling approval and a few car horns joined in.

"Save Dogwood Park for the children!"

"Toot . . . toot-toot-toot . . . toot-toot-toot-toot!"

Despite the blurrings of movement and sound, Gracie thought she could still hear above the din Gillian's triumphant *"Yes!"*

5

I TELL YOU," GILLIAN EXULTED, "our friend here is a born activist!"

Gracie looked abashed. Lacey patted her arm supportively. Used to her grandmother's grandstanding, she might have recognized that not every middle-aged female longed to play the Joan of Arc role. In Lacey's experience, Gracie was about comfort, not upheaval.

She smiled, winking at Gracie. Meanwhile, her grandmother held forth on their visitor's unexpected triumph.

"I'll warrant they would have followed her anywhere!"

In a softer tone, but with the certainty of a prophet, she said, "And they still will, Gracie Parks! Mark my words! Now, someone pass those tacos before they get cold!"

Gracie, despite her answering smile, felt a chill between her shoulder blades. *I never set out to be an activist, Lord,* she reminded Him, *or any other kind of "ist," as far as that goes. But then, probably John the Baptist didn't, either—and if this is the way You're leading me, well . . .* she shivered again. *But I think I'd really rather You wouldn't.*

There were five of them around the table—not counting Gooseberry, who was not around it but under it, warming Gracie's feet.

Lacey's grandmother, along with her fiery activism, had an artistic bent. Gracie learned that she didn't cook—the food in her home was almost always carry-out—but, still, all her meals were served in lovely china platters and bowls. An arrangement of early-blooming iris and soft ferns brightened the table.

As the tray began its second trip, Lacey explained, "This is Gram's 'Iris Room.' It started because of the carving at the mantel. See?" She paused while Gracie obediently looked.

Tall spires of iris had been chiseled into the fireplace's wooden frame. Deep channels outlined the flowers' stems, dense, curved foliage and heavy blooms.

Gracie wondered how many generations of small fingertips had smoothed the carvings to their current gleam, how many decades of firelit nights had blackened them past any semblance of springtime.

Lacey seemed to tune into her thoughts as she continued, "Even way back when Gram was little, they popped corn here in a funny metal box with a sliding top door and a long, long handle! Can you imagine?"

Gracie certainly could.

"Then Gram found the iris umbrella stand and carpet at an antique auction—" Lacey paused. "But the very, very, *very* best is the stained-glass window! Don't you think?"

It truly was beautiful—actually a panel, tall and narrow, set within the existing window. Its vibrant purples, blues and greens evoked the very essence of spring.

"And when the sun shines," Lacey said, "like, especially in the morning, then it's just wonderful in here, too." She reached to catch Gracie's hand. "And Gracie, guess what! *He* made it!" She pointed at Deke Brandt, who made a modest, self-deprecating face.

"I knew you were an artist." Gracie shook her head in admiration, "but—"

"Oh, Deke can do anything!" Lacey said proudly. "We're really lucky he found us, aren't we, Aunt Kelly?"

Kelly blushed. Then she looked at Deke with the same pride her niece was displaying.

The ringing of the telephone suddenly interrupted Gillian, who was about to say something.

"Oh, no!" cautioned Kelly. "It could be the anonymous caller again! He usually interrupts meals," she explained to Gracie.

All at the table were silent as Gillian listened, her lips tightening. Finally she said firmly, "Sir—whoever you are—if and when you're prepared to discuss this in a respectful manner, I'll be happy to talk with you. Face to face."

She paused. "But, please remember, I don't respond to threats."

Lacey had insisted she be the one to show Gracie to the room where she would stay. "It's called 'The Safari Room,' and you'll see why when we get there."

She took three excited skipping steps as she led the way and, as a result, Gracie's smaller bag, which Lacey carried, listed dangerously. Gracie could imagine a tidal wave of mouthwash engulfing her face cream. Oh, well. Nothing short of finding a tarantula curled in her bed could destroy her anticipation of a good night's rest. Thank goodness she'd noticed no bananas!

And I won't worry about Uncle Miltie, she assured the Lord. *I know he's in the best of hands—Yours. Tonight I plan to curl up between cool sheets and simply enjoy being a cozy guest in a good friend's house.*

Gooseberry, bounding ahead, seemed to agree.

"Gooseberry will always protect you! He's one big cat!" Lacey regarded Gracie's pet with respect.

"*Mmm.*" Gracie wasn't certain of Gooseberry's bravery in all instances.

"But the nice thing is you protect each other." Before Gracie could respond, she added happily, "Like Aunt Kelly and Deke and me."

Gracie was poised to praise God for the new stability and contentment in this orphaned child's life—and Kelly's—when Lacey slowly opened the door and switched on the light.

"Ta-da!" Lacey sang, standing aside for Gracie to absorb the full effect.

Gracie let her suitcase thump to the carpet—actually a kind of artificial grass—and, looking around, she felt her mouth fall open.

The bed was covered in a paw-printed spread pulled back to reveal a zebra-striped sheet and pillow shams. The walls, she registered, were patterned in a maze of intricately twined tropical vines with brilliantly colored blossoms and immense leaves. In a wide frieze running around the room at the juncture of ceiling and wall, monkeys sauntered, swung, danced and turned somersaults.

Gracie took a moment before risking a look up at the ceiling itself.

"Stars," Lacey said, as though reading her thoughts. "When the lights are out, you'll see stars all over." She gestured around the room. "You'll think you're right in the jungle, all night long!"

That's just what Gracie was afraid of!

She was only glad there were no jungle sound effects.

There was, however, a kneeling elephant roughly the size of a steamer trunk.

"Of course the tusks aren't real. You just use them for hanging your stuff." Lacey gestured to a spot of wildly patterned wall behind a bamboo rocking chair. "But he makes a better clothesrack."

He? Gracie wasn't certain she was prepared for another inhabitant of this room in addition to Gooseberry and herself.

The giraffe was as nearly life-sized as the room would allow. With spindly legs wide-braced, he seemed awkwardly bent over about to take a cool drink from a stream.

The artisan who had carved him had taken great pains. He was as beautiful as he was unexpected.

"Did Deke—?" Gracie began.

"No. But he's going to make a lion family. Though I can't think where Gram will find room!"

Without pausing, Lacey added, "I like to sit here." She settled onto a low bench. "And I have conversations with my giraffe sometimes, just like you do with God."

"Well, I hope sometimes you talk to God, too."

"I do," Lacey replied simply.

"Is this usually your room, then?" Gracie was willing to surrender her temporary guest's claim.

"Oh, no. I sleep in the Angel Room." Lacey bounded up, giving the giraffe a parting hug. "Want to see it?"

"I think I'm too tired, dear."

Gooseberry yawned helpfully.

"In fact, both of us are very tired. And tomorrow will be an even busier day."

"The wedding practice!" Lacey sighed, hugging Gracie. "*Oooooh*, we're so glad you decided to come!"

THE NEXT MORNING, Gracie found Gillian in the kitchen stacking perfect pancakes from styrofoam take-out containers. The plastic syrup packets were piled into a rough-textured pottery bowl.

"Deke isn't here yet," she greeted Gracie. "Did you sleep well? The wildlife in your room didn't disturb your sleep? Those are species not native to Indiana!"

Gracie was grateful that Gillian was so naturally chatty. As it had been her first night in a strange bed, with a host of jungle creatures looking on, she had awakened with an unaccustomed headache. And it wasn't easy to hold up her end of the conversation because of it.

Gooseberry, on the other hand, had slept deeply and noisily. She'd never have imagined he'd be so at home in such menacing surroundings—after all, as Gillian had said, jungles were scarce in Willow Bend and environs. He'd never met a giraffe before!

"You're all right, dear?" Gillian, finished with the pancake-stacking, now stopped to observe Gracie's slightly strained countenance.

Gracie smiled, determined not to complain. She was sure she'd feel better as the morning went on.

Gillian set a frosted pitcher and a tower of glasses on the sideboard while she cracked a tray of ice cubes. "I hope you like your juice cold. Help yourself, dear."

Gracie tried to look thirsty, but now her head suddenly was thudding like a battered old engine.

"Oh, my dear—you truly don't seem well!" Gillian came over and pressed her hand against Gracie's forehead. "Your skin feels normal, thank goodness." She peered at Gracie reassuringly.

"A walk," Gracie said. "I think . . . if I could get some fresh air—" She stood up slowly.

"Of course! And I'll go with you! Just to make sure you don't get lost."

But Gooseberry, appearing from nowhere, purred at Gracie's ankles, asserting his prior claim.

"We'll be fine." Gracie forced a smile. "You've got a lot to do here."

"If you should get lost," Deke's voice came through the open door, "just look for the mountain of new picket signs."

He walked into the kitchen, stooping briefly to pet Gooseberry.

"New signs?" Gillian turned as she finished pouring the juice. "Where?"

"Come and see," he replied.

Gillian shooed Gracie and Gooseberry ahead.

A dozen large signs on smoothly sanded poles had appeared in the night and now leaned against the porch railing. Some oval, others rectangular, they were lettered in elaborate Victorian style in maroon, greens and blues.

"Lightweight, but sturdy." Deke handed one each to Gracie and Gillian. Through headache-blurred eyes, Gracie saw that hers carried her own legend: SAVE DOGWOOD PARK FOR THE CHILDREN!

For a moment or so, Gillian was uncharacteristically wordless. Then she enveloped her son-in-law to-be in a giant hug. "Deke, you wonderful man! Whenever did you find the time?"

He held up his hand in protest as he extricated himself. "I didn't mean to give the impression it was me! I haven't even a clue who made them!"

"You didn't?" Gillian frowned. "But you must have! Who else . . . ?"

Grinning, he shrugged. "Your guess is probably better than mine." He sniffed the air. "Pancakes? I'm starving!" He opened the door for the two women.

As Deke began to serve himself pancakes, Gracie and

Gooseberry excused themselves and headed out on their walk. After just a minute or two, Gracie began to feel more focused. More like herself.

What is there about exercise, Lord, that limbers up the brain cells as fully as the leg muscles? Pure fresh air can be as good as any prescription! What a marvelous world You've created—and what wonderful people! I do like that young man Deke! But who could have crafted those lovely placards and left them there if it wasn't he?

She returned in her memory to the day Arlen and Wendy, hand in hand, had confided to her their intention to marry. *It would have been disappointing, Lord, if she hadn't been able to accept me as another mother. It looks like Deke and Gillian already have that closeness. Thank You!*

Gooseberry, tail high, trotted next to her. There were new yards to sniff. He seemed to enjoy fresh discoveries without carrying the baggage of old ones. And he cared very little about the intricacies of human relationships.

Gracie was familiar with more of Mason City than the courthouse. She remembered attending summer concerts there with El, then topping off the evening with a sundae at the Mercantile Ice Cream and Soda Shoppe. Before Willow Bend had become more self-sufficient—with such additions as Abe's Deli—the county seat had seemed simply an extension of home. Now, when she and Uncle Miltie went, it classified as a mini-excursion.

Suddenly, looking around, she realized Gooseberry had

taken a route into seedier areas. She sighed to see the decay of small buildings all around them and the general disinterest in paint and repair. In one doorway a man stood, leaning unsteadily.

Oh, dear Lord, what tragedies have brought him here?

"Well, now, kitty, and who might you be?" The fellow beckoned to her wandering feline.

His voice was not slurred, nor was it rough, as she might have supposed. *Forgive me, Lord, and help me not to judge my fellow creatures by their appearances.*

Stroking Gooseberry, he continued speaking to the cat in tones that sounded cultured, even slightly theatrical.

Gooseberry—eyes closed in bliss—accepted the steady massage.

"Like that, do you?" The man looked up then, with eyes that were clear gray and intelligent. "Ma'am, do you belong to him or he to you?" Without waiting for an answer, he chuckled. "You're a matched set. Kitty here the color of Halloween pumpkins, and your hair—" He shook his head, as though the color of her coiffure defied description.

Gracie broke an awkward silence by suggesting to Gooseberry that they move on.

"Are you a citizen of Mason City somehow unknown to me?"

"No. I'm here to visit a friend." Gracie hesitated. "Gillian Pomeroy."

He grinned with surprised approval. "The town character," he chuckled. "Though it's possible she'd have the same to say of me." He waved as Gracie and Gooseberry turned to retrace their footsteps back to the Pomeroy house.

When they encountered Gillian, now tidying up in the kitchen, her response was exactly as the stranger had predicted. "Darius Plunkett," she declared. "He's a local eccentric."

Gracie hoped for more details and looked encouragingly at Gillian to continue.

"Professor Plunkett, as he's sometimes called, teaches the occasional class at Avery Junior College," her hostess explained. "He's often charming, but sometimes not."

"Well, he was courtly today, if nothing else."

"He's a fraud—though he means no harm to anyone, as far as I know. If you saw him clutching a bottle, it probably held iced tea. He fancies himself a tourist attraction, it seems—but the seedy derelict role is only one of the many he likes to play."

Gracie looked at Gillian. His performance, to her at least, had seemed pretty convincing.

"You see, he's had theatrical experience. Rumor has it he did some touring as an actor. For real. A real actor, I mean. Oh, and he's had a couple of books published. But that doesn't mean I've ever read one of them."

Gracie thought of Anna Searfoss, Willow Bend's only author. Before diabetes had impaired her sight, Anna had authored and illustrated a series of children's books. But she was totally without pretense.

Gracie said, "In Willow Bend, what you see is what you get, and once I stop to think about it, that's a good thing. I don't want my neighbor to be a cowboy one day and a tap dancer the next. Consistency counts."

Gillian declared, "My problem with Darius Plunkett is, he's not really serious enough. Writing books is one thing, but what counts for me is helping rewrite the laws so things turn out as they ought to!"

Gillian seemed lost in thought for a moment. "He is, or could be, a fine figure of a man, I'll give him that."

NOW I WANT US to keep it simple," Kelly said.

She was looking very pretty, Gracie thought, with her hair swept up and curly little strands straying past her ears.

Noting the current easy camaraderie exhibited by Gillian, Kelly and Lacey, Gracie had to struggle to recall the once seemingly irreparable rents their relationship had survived. *Thank You, Lord. It does seem—doesn't it—that few of us are ever able to learn to accept life's best fruits without first sampling its thistles and poison ivy.*

"Hors d'oeuvres," pronounced Gillian, pen poised over a notepad.

"Chocolate-covered strawberries." Lacey spoke each syllable as though she were tasting it. *"Yum."*

Laughing, Kelly hugged her niece.

"Chocolate-covered strawberries," Gillian repeated as she

wrote it down. "But those are more like dessert. How about stuffed mushrooms?"

"*Hmm*," Kelly said. "Let me think a moment."

"I could help!" offered Lacey. "What do you stuff them with?"

"Not chocolate!" teased Kelly. "I'd like those little spinach pies, maybe. But probably a beautiful platter of crudités and dip would be fine, and also less filling."

"I can do both with no trouble," Gracie told them, making the beginning of a shopping list.

"Then for the buffet, a variety of salads—slaw, potato, macaroni, broccoli, Jell-o—and for the meats, ham and chicken wings."

Gracie suggested, "Honey mustard, barbequed, lemon pepper—"

"That's enough! We want to—"

"—keep it simple!" Lacey and Gillian chorused, and Kelly laughed, blushing.

"Maybe it's already past simple?"

Lacey protested, "You still need wedding cake! That's the absolute most important thing!"

"Don't worry, honey," said her grandmother. "We wouldn't ever forget the cake!"

"I have an idea!" Kelly announced with a smile. "Why don't we all go for ice cream sundaes? We deserve a reward! All this list-making and so many decisions—it's like work!"

"Dear . . . ," Gillian began.

"I know," Kelly told her. "You have to go to the beauty parlor. We'll walk you there afterwards, okay?"

Lacey's vote on the ice cream issue was not in doubt. Seeing her excitement, Gillian agreed to the plan.

But she turned to her daughter with a pleading expression. "I could skip the hairdresser's. I have some material to organize at my desk."

"It's settled," Kelly said firmly. "Your appointment's made, and it's my wedding! This way, you can get used to having it styled and decide exactly how you want it for the wedding. We're calling this a trial run!"

"Yes, ma'am," Gillian said with what might have passed for meekness to those who didn't know her well.

"Yea, Gram!" Lacey was off her seat. "Can I have a chocolate cherry sundae with extra whipped cream and sprinkles?"

Kelly asked teasingly, "Is there any other kind?"

The Mason City Mercantile Ice Cream and Soda Shoppe offered a nearly pristine nineteenth-century interior. Its ceiling alone was enough to extract delighted *ahs* from old-time architecture buffs. Comprised of large intricately patterned tin squares, it stretched high above the glory that was the original marble-topped counter.

Two ancient Coke machines still dispensed soft drinks in glass bottles. The cash register was elaborately scrolled and polished to a gleaming brilliance. And on the wooden shelves that ran along the shop's center aisle, there were antiques of every description, from old mixing bowls to toy instruments.

Lacey picked up a faded tambourine and shook it gaily, causing her aunt and grandmother to smile. She twirled around.

Perched on a high wrought-iron stool, Gracie felt, of all things, an unexpected tug of concern for Uncle Miltie. *Is it You, Lord—and if so, what would You have me know?* The nudge might have been triggered by the presence of sundaes, sodas, toppings, maraschino cherries and all the other manifestations of one of Uncle Miltie's favorite foods: ice cream, in all its sweet and gooey glory.

Or was it simply that Marian Jones, the Mercantile's genial proprietress, asked after him. "I know he's your uncle—and how can I forget his corny jokes?" she told Gracie. "I just can't recall his name!"

"George Morgan," Gracie answered, "but he goes by the nickname, Uncle Miltie."

"Because of the jokes." Lacey added, noisily slurping a spoonful of sundae.

"You know, Milton Berle," explained Gillian, "the TV comic—"

"I remember Milton Berle!"

Gracie protested, "You're not old enough!"

"Thanks, Gracie," said Marian.

Voices swirled around, but Gracie's thoughts had shifted. She should have insisted that Uncle Miltie call as soon as he arrived in Pittsburgh. The problem, since her departure coincided with his, was that she'd had too much on her mind.

Though she had the telephone number of his Army buddy, she wasn't certain even of his name. What *had* she been thinking? He was bound to be okay, but he was *her* responsibility and she'd gotten used to making certain of his well-being. It just came naturally to her, even though he often thought it unnecessary.

Lord, will I ever truly achieve the level of faith I like to think I already possess? It's relatively easy to have it about the little things, the daily things, but in times of trouble or worry, when faith is most required, when Yours should be the first help I reach for—why do I insist on taking the weight upon myself?

For another moment she sat with her heart reaching and her spirit quieting as she waited for guidance. Then, strengthened, she knew what to do. She'd call that very night, and if Uncle Miltie or his friend thought her a fussbudget, so be it.

Harriet's Hair Salon was located on the ground floor of a building facing the now star-spangled rear view of General Alistair Mason's mount. Repainting the horse had been an act of clever daring, Gracie thought as she registered the gaudy outcome once again.

"You're really going to force me to do this, aren't you?"

Gillian sighed. "I've been avoiding hairdresser's for several decades now!"

Kelly responded by taking her mother's arm and urging her toward the glass-fronted shop. "Mom normally trims her own hair," Kelly explained, and Gracie nodded, unsurprised.

"I always have. And yours, too, Kelly dear."

Kelly made a face. Lacey looked at her curiously.

Gillian regarded her daughter. "Are you telling me now you wish I hadn't?"

Kelly hesitated.

"Were you ashamed of it? Of . . . me?"

"Never you, Mom." Kelly's tone was wry. "Mom, I don't want to hurt your feelings—it's just that sometimes bowl cuts weren't exactly the latest style."

"I understand," Gillian told her. "I can be stubborn, and you've been a wonderful daughter to put up with me. Even when you did things I didn't approve of, I never doubted your love."

Gracie watched them stop and hug each other. At the same time, she couldn't help but be amazed that such a strong person could make such a fuss about a simple haircut and set. Lacey danced around them, and they all hugged.

"Gram, you look great to me now," the girl said solemnly. "But I can't wait to see how you'll look when you're done here!"

Harriet Langhorne's shop was of the sort found in most small towns. A bit fancier than Willow Bend's two beauty parlors, it nonetheless felt like home to Gracie.

Lacey sat down with Kelly at a wicker table scattered with magazines. None of them, Gracie noted, were copies of *Guideposts*. She'd have to send them a subscription, as she'd long-ago done with her most-frequented Willow Bend establishments; happily, all of them now kept their own subscriptions current.

Gracie wondered idly if it might not be wise to have her own roots touched up before the wedding. It might even be relaxing to spend a couple of hours sitting still under someone else's ministrations.

While Kelly moved to the appointment table to report her mother's arrival on time, Gillian stood by the coat-rack, looking as if she would like to escape.

"Gram looks like she'd like to be anywhere but here!" Lacey declared as she watched her grandmother being led to the shampooing area.

Joining them, Kelly patted Lacey's shoulder. "Don't worry about her. She's walked picket lines in freezing rain, shared a homeless family's cardboard box on Christmas Eve, and has been carried in a police van to a cold prison cell with only her determination to give her comfort. My guess is she'll manage to survive this, too."

Lacey sat quietly. Around her, women chatted, dryers

whirred and whined, and chairs squeaked. She cleared her throat. "Aunt Kelly—"

Kelly paused in the act of turning a page in the magazine on her lap. "*Hmm?*"

"Do you think— Uh, you don't think Gram's ... silly ... do you?"

Kelly considered the question for less than a second before replying. "Lacey, I think she's the most amazing, unusual, courageous, wonderful—"

And that was when the first of a series of screams froze all activity in the room.

First making certain that Gillian was safe, gracie scanned the faces of the other women within view, hoping to discern the cause of the uproar. Gillian, a silver-blue plastic cape cascading over her shoulders, seemed alert—poised to act if necessary.

Lacey smiled with relief. "Gram's okay. Look, she's worried about everyone else, like always."

It suddenly became easy to identify the screamer, and the reason for her distress was equally obvious: The woman's hair was fluorescent fuschia. On a clown, it would be snazzy; on a Mason City lady of a certain age and certain size, it was bound to be deeply distressing.

The young hairdresser who strove to calm her customer also seemed to be on the verge of screaming herself. Her face was a mask of shock and concern. The offending bottle of color splashed its murky liquid to the floor.

For a few moments, a sense of calm came over the room. But not for long. Soon came a scream in a deeper key— contralto, Gracie surmised—and then a mezzo-soprano. For a crazy moment, Gracie could think of nothing but Estelle Livett, her choir's temperamental diva, hitting high D.

"Wow!" Lacey's eyes were wide. "Look! Blue! And there's *green*! And . . . and purple! It's like a paint-box made of people!"

Sitting near her, a young manicurist wore an unreadable expression.

"Wow!" exhaled Lacey. "Wow!"

I should do something, Lord, Gracie thought, but what? What kind of rescue squad should be summoned for a bevy of indignant women striving only to conceal their graying locks? Gracie could only marvel at the effects of pandemonium in such a small space.

Lord, can't You do something? Are You waiting for me?

At that moment, an authority figure of just the sort needed managed to get everyone's attention. "What's the meaning of this?" she demanded.

"That's Harriet Langhorne," Kelly observed. "She earned a bronze star in Vietnam."

The coming of Harriet Langhorne obviated the necessity

for an outside rescue team. Her "Ladies, enough!" was suffi-
cient to restore some order.

The fuschia coiffure was sobbing quietly. Her purple companion in distress clutched the phone, declaring her intention
to call her lawyer. Madame Blue, turning her head from side
to side as she studied her reflection, seemed rather intrigued
by her startling transformation, and Greenie still sat stunned.

Once again commanding everyone's attention, Harriet
Langhorne said, "Ladies, everything's under control. Truly.
Someone has an unfortunate sense of humor, that's all. I'm
sure the dye— er, color—is washable. So if you four who've
been affected will allow us to work with you, we should have
your natural colors restored in moments."

She turned. "Glynnis!"

The manicurist stood. "Yes, Mama?" Her expression,
Gracie thought, was hard to read.

"Can you take a few moments to help with the rinses?"

"Of course." Glynnis stood up obediently.

Soon the newly colorful quartet had been restored to their
old selves. *Hair today, gone tomorrow,* as Uncle Miltie undoubtedly would quip, thought Gracie. Or maybe he'd dub it
"hair-esy."

"Done!" Gillian stood before them, her silver mane tamed
into a flattering wave. "Even I have to admit it looks pretty
nice."

"Wow, Gram!" breathed Lacey. "You're beautiful!"

"Thank you, darling," Gillian replied, obviously pleased. "I'm sure when I come back next week they won't be able to guarantee such an afternoon's excitement! For a moment, I thought we might need those riot police I used to know so well."

Watching her as they strolled out of Harriet's Hair Salon, Gracie could swear Gillian Pomeroy looked almost wistful.

8

"YOU WOULDN'T BELIEVE IT, DEKE!" Lacey insisted. "It was better than a movie! With special effects, even!"

They were eating that night in Gillian's Victorian Room. But, in fact, Gracie thought, the room was only predominantly Victorian. There were also scattered touches of Art Deco, Early American and even Danish Modern. Amazingly, it all blended.

If Gillian Pomeroy had not carried out a career as a social activist, Gracie was certain, she could have made a fortune as an innovative decorator.

"Let me point out a few of my favorite pieces," Gillian said. "The carved wooden figurehead is from a clipper ship that sank off the coast of Maine. Do you remember that old poem 'The Wreck of the Hesperus'? Mother used to recite it to us when we were young, declaiming it while she made the best raised doughnuts in the world. I still remember sobbing, my heart broken for the Captain's little daughter, lashed to the mast. The antique dealer who sold this to me swore that this figurehead was part of the very ship."

She gave a merry hoot of laughter. "Fortunately, I'm not that gullible. But I do love its chipping paint and roughened surface. It's an object that has real character—one that's seen the vicissitudes of life and still survived to be here."

"Like you, Gram," Lacey said with admiration. "You've survived viciss— viciss'tudes, too."

Deke ruffled her hair. "Don't use words you don't understand, Peanut," he teased.

"It means—" Lacey struggled for a second for a plausible definition. "Storms and stuff," she finished triumphantly. "Right, Gram?"

"Good save!" Deke said. "You think on your feet, Lacey, honey, and that ability should serve you well."

Lacey grinned sheepishly. "I didn't *really* know. But I thought it had to have something to do with the ocean."

He laughed. "Better quit while you're ahead!"

For a time they ate in silence. There was more detail in the room than Gracie could take in, admire it as she might. It wasn't to her taste, but Gillian obviously had a flair for the dramatic.

The meal, however, was more mundane than the setting in which it was served. It was fried-chicken takeout, and there were hot biscuits that even Gracie had to admit were tasty.

Deke commented, "No boar's head complete with apple, I see. But that would be medieval, I suppose, not Victorian!"

"Deke!" warned Kelly.

Gillian added dryly, "It seems that someone else should quit while he's ahead."

They all laughed.

This is nice, Gracie assured the Lord comfortably. *There's evidence of love around this table, and it's as richly textured as all the trimmings in this room. I don't pretend to understand Gillian! You'd think someone with her social goals and uncompromising positions would be more ascetic in her taste! But, Lord, You specialize in marvelous contradictions, don't You? Now, if only I can talk with Uncle Miltie later, so I can stop worrying about him, everything will be perfect.*

There'd been no answer so far the three times she'd tried. All she'd heard was a gruff message: "You've reached the answering machine of Clint Whitley, for all the good it's done you. The trout are running, for one thing. For another, I can't abide these contraptions! So get yourself a rod and bait and join me, if you want—but don't bother to leave a message. I don't care to hear it."

So far she hadn't had the courage to leave even a greeting for Uncle Miltie. But eventually she would, no matter how it might rile the seemingly misanthropic Mr. Whitley. Besides, the poor man had had a hospital stay and was probably going to be crankier than ever, recuperating. Uncle Miltie had assured her it was only something minor, but Clint Whitley had had the good sense to know he needed a friend nearby.

"This is so great," Lacey said, interrupting Gracie's thoughts. "Us. Together, being happy."

Gracie couldn't help but feel a lump in her throat. She forgot her anxiety about Uncle Miltie as she looked at these happy people.

Deke caught Lacey's hand in one of his and Kelly's in the other. "We can't promise we won't have sadness," he said gently, "or even that we'll always be together. But what we can promise is that we'll always love one another. And yes, that you can count on."

Gracie's lump got bigger. She swallowed again and blinked away a tear.

The silence that fell was nearly reverent, Gracie felt, and she found herself asking the Lord to bless them all. She knew He would.

"Well," Gillian said at last. Her voice was husky. "Lacey, dear, if you'll blow out the candles, and Deke, if you can find the light switch, Kelly and I will clear the table, and we'll finish this lovely evening with a vicious game of Monopoly."

LACEY SUCCUMBED FIRST TO an attack of the yawns.

"A good thing, too." Deke glowered at the game board. "I was about to go to debtors' prison."

Lacey giggled. "You can stay in one of my hotels—but not on Park Place. Or maybe in a caboose, attached to one of my railroads!"

Kelly stretched her arms. "My niece the financier! In my old age she'll keep me in luxury!"

Deke looked crestfallen. "I thought I was going to do that!"

Kelly indicated his slim Monopoly holdings. "Not likely."

He leaned back, hands behind his head, a lazy smile playing on his lips. "So you're not going to answer the 'richer or poorer' part of the wedding ceremony? Just clear your throat or something?"

Kelly considered. "Would 'no comment' work?"

Lacey yawned more widely. "I'll lend you money, Deke. Or I would, if I had any."

"Right now," Kelly said firmly, "you're going to bed, young lady. And Deke's going home."

Deke stood. "That's the way it is, when you lose your wealth."

"My pauper prince." Kelly gave him a quick kiss. "See you tomorrow. Maybe Gracie will give you a job folding napkins. The pay's not great, but you can have all the napkins you can eat."

Later, when all was quiet, the game pieces were stored, and only Gracie and Gillian remained at the table—a teapot between them—Gillian said gently, "They're marvelous together, aren't they?"

"Perfect." Gracie sipped her tea thoughtfully. *Where can Uncle Miltie be, Lord? Why can't I reach him?* Unbidden, he had returned to her thoughts.

"No answer again?" Gillian reached out her hand in comfort.

"Only that cantankerous message! And I'm just not sure when that old coot is going in for his surgery. It's not a big deal, really, Uncle Miltie gave me to think. An out-patient thing—though, at his age, some extra observation time could be called for."

"But you may just be calling in between the times they're

there. Despite his threats not to, Uncle Miltie's friend may actually be checking the messages on his machine. He sounds, really, as if hot air may be just his style!"

"I haven't left one. At least, not yet," Gracie admitted.

"Well!" Gillian exclaimed. "Gracie Parks intimidated! Never thought I'd see the day!"

Gracie defended herself. "Mr. Whitley seems so determined to call the shots. He was cautious enough to ask for Uncle Miltie's companionship. I don't feel right trying to tread on his privacy."

Gillian thought a moment. "Well, your uncle's a big boy, and perhaps you're being overprotective. Maybe he's just savoring his freedom from routine, no matter how much he loves living with you in Willow Bend."

"I realize I'm being silly." Gracie brushed back a stray curl.

"You love him."

"Oh, yes," Gracie agreed. She had adored her Uncle George and Aunt Doris from the time she could climb into their welcoming laps. In large part, it had been this dear man who'd fostered her appreciation of nature, teaching her to listen to the voices of chipmunks and cicadas, the conversation of pines and breeze, the music of water in all its moods. She had loved her summertime visits to the Morgans' comfortable house.

And it had been her uncle, always an avid gardener, who had first shown her how dirt might produce more than mudpies, how it could be coaxed to reproduce the full variety of God's green creations. With Aunt Doris, there had been the lively shared cooking and the happy clatter of utensils. Uncle Miltie had taught a curious child the wonder of quietness.

The joke was, he was so rarely quiet himself these days, or at least that would be the verdict if you asked any of the good citizens of Willow Bend.

Suddenly Gracie found herself saying, "All those years, when he was in his prime, he didn't need me to babysit him. He gave me so much, and he still does."

"All those years, remember, he was much younger. He's still a source of emotional connection, but he's bound to have diminished capabilities!"

Gracie sighed. "That's supposed to make me feel better?"

"No, Gracie. But you do need to be honest about what's worrying you. Uncle Miltie is full of life and intelligence, and humor, but he is a man in his eighties. That's all. You're right to be concerned. Just keep things in perspective."

She's right, Lord, and the perspective I keep everything in is shaped by You. You know where Uncle Miltie is. Please make sure he stays safe—and nudge him to get in touch with his worrywart niece.

"Still no answer?" Gillian asked gently.

"I'll try again in the morning. Surely then—"

"I'm certain of it! Now, about tomorrow. . . ."

"We can shop for everything but the spoilables. I thought maybe Lacey would like to help."

"She'll be ecstatic!" It was Gillian's turn to frown. "I just hope . . . nothing happens to ruin Kelly's special day." She sighed. "You know, I didn't even begin to worry until today."

Today. Gracie replayed the past hours. Oh! The fiasco at the beauty salon. How could she have forgotten so quickly?

And those threatening calls! With her fingers in so many causes and protests, Gillian Pomeroy was a woman with more than a tiny list of enemies.

Gracie asked carefully, "What do you think might happen?"

Gillian shrugged. "Who can say? Until today, the pranks seemed innocuous. I mean, General Mason's horse needed some sprucing up. So what if he's not meant to be spotted? And Mrs. McQuaid—if she'd really looked at her fence— would have thanked the artist. Now that it's been repainted, her place once again looks like all the rest on that street. And those signs—if they were done by the same person—are beautiful! We have another rally planned for tomorrow—had I told you that?"

No, she hadn't. Surely she wouldn't expect Gracie to participate! Not with all she had to do to prepare for the wedding events!

"Where will you be? Protesting, I mean," Gracie said.

"Where will *we* be, you mean! Gracie Parks, we need you for our spark again!"

Before her guest could protest, Gillian said, "As for all the wedding preparations, we'll help out with anything you get behind on. The thing is, not until today was there even a hint of malice!"

Gracie went over in her mind the series of pranks that she'd been told about and also witnessed. Whatever Gillian's excesses, at heart she was a woman of courage, conviction and common sense. That she was concerned at all meant that there was reason to be.

Soberly, Gracie's hostess went on, "What if one of those women at Harriet's had had a heart attack right there? After they looked at themselves in the mirror? I don't know CPR, do you?"

Actually, Gracie, Uncle Miltie and several other friends had taken a refresher course just a few months ago. But she had hoped never to have to put her knowledge to use. Besides, the doughty Gillian didn't require an answer. What she wanted—no, needed!—was reassurance. Amazing, but true.

Gracie started to offer it but before she could say anything, Gillian asserted, "Like it or not, Kelly's not going to have her hair done there for the wedding! It's too risky. Best if we could spirit her away to one of the other nearby towns. What about Willow Bend?"

Gracie ventured, "There's a nice little beauty parlor I go to. I'd be glad to take her."

Gillian looked at Gracie's bright red curls.

"Really," she assured Gillian. "I wouldn't mind a bit. And she wouldn't come out looking like me, I promise."

"It's certainly an idea." Gillian pulled herself together and stood abruptly. "It's time we get some sleep! Tomorrow is going to be a very full day!"

She caught Gracie in a quick hug. "Sleep well, my friend. I know what you'd say: Let God work on our problems for us. He takes the night shift, too."

Long after Gracie lay between her zebra-striped sheets— with a whole galaxy of stars blazing overhead, and with Gooseberry wedged by her side—Gracie considered the mystery of the painted horse, fence and posters and the puzzle of the hair dye.

It can't be the same perpetrator, can it, Lord? The M.O.'s wrong. She smiled, wondering how well versed the good Lord was in the jargon of police procedure. If He watched TV and read mystery novels as she did. . . .

Turning her cheek to her pillow, she began to count monkeys. Beside her, the bundle of fur that was Gooseberry loudly snored and kicked a little.

"Uncle Miltie, wherever you are," she murmured sleepily, "if you could see this room, I'd probably never hear the end of your Tarzan jokes!"

10

AS IT HAPPENED, Gracie wouldn't have missed the demonstration the next day for—as her mother had often said—"all the tea in China."

"Well," Gillian was taking a break from the distribution of picket signs, "what do you think?"

Gracie shook her head. It was clear to her that here in Mason City, Indiana, the veneer of civilization was still in place—but only barely—as the opposing factions showed up to take a stand.

The Mason City high school playing field adjoined the disputed Dogwood Park. It also was in danger of disappearing, as it turned out. Actually, a change might offer an improvement, Gracie thought.

The unpainted wooden bleachers swayed alarmingly with every movement, the billboards bordering the field might have been painted a generation or so ago, and holes and hillocks dotted the baseball diamond itself.

However, she noted with interest, the bases were in great shape—thanks, no doubt, to the phantom artist. She could see only home plate clearly from where she stood, but its surface gleamed with an intricate patriotic design.

"Testing, one, two, three . . . testing, one, two, three. . . ."

Someone spoke at Gracie's shoulder. "I wonder why originality never seems the strong suit of the folks who check out sound systems."

Gracie turned, smiling.

The man looked vaguely familiar. Tall and dressed in neat blue jeans, he wore an open-collared rust-colored shirt and a tweed jacket with leather elbow patches. She caught the light scent of a spicy shaving lotion she'd often bought El—not because it was his own favorite, but because she loved it on him. His last bottle, nearly empty, still sat on her dresser. Somehow, it seemed wrong that she smell it elsewhere. The fragrance should have been retired—like a football jersey—at his death.

She frowned. *Where have I met this man before? I remember the voice, but the face is unfamiliar. And if he'd been wearing the shaving lotion then, I could never have forgotten.*

It was when the stranger said, "I see that your hostess is spearheading the event. No one throws a protest like Gillian Pomeroy!" that she remembered Darius Plunkett.

"Isn't that—" Gracie looked across the park and struggled for the name she had seen often beneath newspaper photos and on local campaign posters.

"Commissioner Tyrone Sanders."

"Oh!" She had even met the man once, but the impression she'd taken away had obviously relegated him to some back corner of her mind. However, she knew he and Gillian had long been antagonists.

"He's hardly my favorite person either," her companion said, moving away.

Idly, Gracie watched to see which faction the professor would join. She was oddly gratified to see him position himself near Gillian's troops.

As the morning progressed, the assembled company divided itself into factions. One group—heavy-set and heavy-breathing—formed a rowdy huddle and chanted:

"Progress always asks a price—

But grabbing our bleachers just ain't nice!"

Former high school athletic stars, and now motivated by nostalgia for their moments of glory, they seemed sincere but somehow pathetic.

Lord, forgive me—but I find myself embarrassed for them. Some of those men must already be grandparents! Yet they act as though those long-ago games when they were teenagers remain the high points of their lives!

She thought of Arlen, how he had darted, woven, and sped triumphantly on the soccer field. But his Most Valuable Player trophy now served as a doorstop in her laundry room. It was work and family today that caused him to glow with pride and to approach God in thanks.

It was soon apparent, however, that not everyone shared Gracie's assessment of Mason City's aging jocks' cause. A flood of fresh supporters now swelled their ranks. Three grandmotherly types in sweatshirts and jeans waved pennants and led the crowd in a Mason City High cheer.

His spicy scent preceded Professor Plunkett's appearance by mere seconds. "Doesn't it strike you as odd, the total lack of alumni supporters under the age of forty-five?"

It was true. The younger people in attendance had attached themselves to Gillian's group. Although more than a few of them wore sweaters with athletic symbols, their support was less for a landmark of local sports history and more for the idea of preservation in general.

Gracie frowned. Was there something about her own generation that rooted them in past glories and made them less clearsighted about the greater communal good?

Gillian, fairly glowing with excitement and purpose, waved at Gracie.

Gracie, waving back, took a moment to debate with herself what Elmo might have thought of all this civic hullabaloo. He had loved sports, certainly. At the same time he frequently declared, "Sports is a part of life—an exciting part—but only a part. And far from the most important."

No, El might see a need for a new stadium—or even repairs to the old one. But he would never have placed that above the greater community served by Dogwood Park. Whether as citizen or as mayor of Willow Bend, his priorities had always rested with the responsible stewardship of God's gifts, which meant ensuring that no groups of citizens—however small— be subjugated to the desires of the more vocal.

Surveying the throng before her in Mason City, Gracie knew in her heart that El would have cast his vote with Gillian and Dogwood Park. And he would have been appalled to see so many spoiling for a fight.

It was not long in coming.

The opening volley occurred when Tyrone Sanders seemed satisfied that the microphone had been sufficiently tested.

"Ladies and gentlemen," he began silkily, "We meet today as a testament to the American way. What a privilege it is to live in a society where anyone—however misguided—has the right—nay, the obligation—to express his or her opinion."

"Blah-blah-blah—" one opponent called, while another yelled, "Get on with it, Sanders! You ain't up for reelection!"

"And you wouldn't get my vote—no how, no way!"

"Nor mine neither!"

"Now, now." The commissioner seemed unruffled. "No need to get personal, is there?"

Disengaging the microphone from its stand, he pulled the cord along the shaky platform as he strode and gestured in exhortation. "There's no question that all are worthy positions represented here!" He waited, but only a spattering of applause resulted.

"First, we have a corps of environmentalists, led by the indomitable Ms. Pomeroy!" He gave a mocking bow in her direction. "This group—while well-meaning, I'm certain— declares with loud certainty that Dogwood Park must be preserved. Ladies and gentlemen, what exactly *is* Dogwood Park? Look about you! Do these unkempt acres protect some endangered species? Spotted owls, perhaps?"

He put his finger to his lips and gave the appearance of close listening. "I hear no owls, spotted, striped or plaid. Siberian tigers, then?"

An uncertain titter could be heard.

"I think not. How about some obscure grub or creeping vine? No! All have been kicked up by little tennis shoes or squirreled away in denim pockets to shrivel up and die."

Again he paused.

"Ms. Pomeroy and her stalwarts would have us believe that the shopping center we propose will leave our town's lively children with nowhere to play. How lacking in vision! Does she fail to understand that playgrounds spring up wherever there are children, dogs and balls to chase after? Let our little ones use their imaginations! Their initiatives! Let there be built here—" he gave an all-encompassing gesture, "stores where parents may conveniently purchase tennis shoes, bats and mitts—all the necessities of play!"

Gracie raised her picket sign, and quickly Gillian's group began to fan across the field, "Save Dogwood Park! Save Dogwood Park!" they chanted with fervor.

One lone voice piped up, "Nothing's wrong with shops! Buy tennis shoes at the new shopping center—get a second pair half-price!"

Almost at once, the alumni contingent stood and shouted, "Down with tennis shoes! Down with Dogwood Park! Save our stadium! Save our stadium!" Most of the attendees, however, were content at that point to stay in their places.

Then one burly man decided to stomp down from the bleacher and attempt to grab a picket sign. Its holder promptly bopped him on the head.

A shoving match seemed about to ensue, but Tyrone Sanders managed to keep hold on the microphone, despite the attempts of a few rivals to grab it.

"Calm down out there!" he insisted. "Violence will achieve nothing but a night in a cold jail cell! There's an obvious solution here! Let the city establish another park, one we can be proud of. And let there be a new stadium—a bigger, better one—closer to the high school!"

Gracie hated to admit it, but he was finally making some sense—especially about the stadium. Now at least two blocks from the school proper, its location necessitated the busing of teams and band members, not to mention equipment, no matter what the season.

"Save Dogwood Park!"

"Save our stadium!"

Like the nimble politician he was, Sanders was ever ready to try another tack. "Friends of our stadium, even though I'm not yet a senior citizen—"

This comment drew a hoot of laughter, which he ignored. "But when I reach that hallowed position in life, I'm certain that I, too, will be committed to nostalgia . . . to those places where, as a barefoot boy, I strove to catch butterflies and fly balls . . . and as I became a teenager . . . to the roar of past crowds, the flush of past glories."

He allowed himself a chuckle.

"Though my own triumphs have been in quite a different arena, I know their glow will illuminate my declining years. But consider, dear friends, do any of you doubt that our present stadium is unsafe? That competing teams find its facilities laughable? And if indeed the ghosts of old cheers hover there, could structural steel and macadam banish them? So when you visit the new mini-mall we intend to build here, you will surely find your memories waiting for you there. . . ."

He had gone too far. In the flush of his oratory, he had preferred the rhythm of his rhetoric to anything that might appease his listeners.

There were three situations that had always puzzled Gracie. One was how, when people could save only a very few items from a burning home, they seldom chose wisely.

The second puzzle pertained to blizzards. How could anyone possibly die only paces from the safety of shelter? (That question, in fact, had been answered dramatically a year before Arlen was born. Caught in a raging snowstorm that obliterated all landmarks, she and Elmo had nearly perished when within sight of an inhabited farmhouse.)

And now, it seemed, in Mason City's Dogwood Park, she would have her third question answered. How could innocent people become enmeshed in a riot?

11

S HE HADN'T SEEN IT COMING.

At a signal, it seemed, the most muscular of the former quarterbacks clumped down from the bleachers, rushed the platform, set Tyrone Sanders none too gently aside, and commandeered the microphone.

"We're talkin' sacrilege here!" he thundered. "A mall? No way! Picture it, guys! Ladies' undies peddled where we suited up and took our after-game showers! Come on, sports fans! Let's hear it!"

Using the microphone as a baton he led the cheer: "Take Dogwood Park! Save our stadium! Save our stadium!"

Now exasperated Gillian Pomeroy somehow heaved herself up and ducked beneath a burly arm to wrest away the mike.

"Please, friends, it's not the park or the stadium that's the problem, it's the plan for the shopping center!" Someone attempted, most rudely, to push her aside.

"You're the problem, lady! Butt out!"

"Let me speak!" Gillian insisted, and, for a brief moment, the force of her passionate sincerity stunned the crowd into silence. But then, with no warning, an ex-football player tackled her, and she went down with an amplified thump, the mike rolling noisily from her reach.

Trying to reclaim it, Tyrone Sanders wound up frustrated enough to unplug it at its source. The next person to capture it tossed it toward Sanders, but unfortunately, his aim was off. A town official, yelping, held his eye and thrashed out with his free fist while the whole platform exploded into a mass of thrashing bodies. Beneath it, the spectators followed suit.

The shouting increased as blows landed, as wood thunked on skulls, as bleachers creaked, groaned, and eventually capsized. And then began a new, thready—thoroughly welcome—sound. Sirens!

For one confused moment, Gracie imagined Herb Bower driving up in his squad car, quelling the disturbance by the authority of his imposing presence as much as by any real display of force.

But this was not Willow Bend. Herb Bower would not be riding to the rescue. Gracie knew she sorely missed him now.

Something bumped her head, and she felt herself sinking.

"Here." Strong hands caught her elbow, and the scent of spiced aftershave wafted near her.

"El . . . ?" she asked weakly. Her head throbbed. Her eyes wouldn't focus properly.

No, of course, it wasn't El.

The noise of the sirens intensified, yet there was no diminishing of shouts and shoves and threats.

Her rescuer said, "No use trying to move." He sounded apologetic.

She took his advice but hadn't the energy to do otherwise, even if she chose.

The sirens whirred into silence. Flashbulbs popped somewhere near them.

"Gracie?"

She turned, slowly. Among the sea of heads, she caught the glint of silver against black. The restless tide of humanity parted to reveal Rocky Gravino.

Gently, he caught her against him. "Dear girl, I never knew catering could be so dangerous!"

Amazing, Gracie thought, the curative power of a large dish of ice cream!

She and Rocky sat at a small round table in the Mercantile. The formica reminded her of Abe's Deli—though his tables were of a different vintage, padded in brilliant red and bound in chrome. These were a delicate blue, with matching seats, and so small in circumference that Rocky's knees crowded hers. The table supports—like the legs and backs of the chairs—were lacy black wrought iron.

Rocky was attacking a banana split from one side, saving the strawberry for last, Gracie noticed as she carefully scooped the chocolate drizzles from the sides of her melting butter pecan. The maraschino cherry and most of her whipped topping lay in the tidal pool rimming the sundae.

Rocky, amazingly, had said little since the police had earlier released Gracie and most of the other noncombatants. He simply seemed grateful to have Gracie in one piece, she thought. That was nice.

Ouch! she winced, touching the goose-egg on her head. "No concussion," the EMT had said, "but if you get sleepy, call us."

She didn't feel sleepy—just weary and frustrated. She should be well into the preparation of hors d'oeuvres and other freezables. How had she ever allowed Gillian to talk her into attending the demonstration?

"I don't understand," Rocky accused, "how you got involved." When she didn't answer, he went on, "none of it—Dogwood Park, the stadium, the shopping center, the whole caboodle—is worth one of those red hairs."

She couldn't help it, she blushed. Rocky grinned.

He took a swipe at his dish. "I mean, Mrs. Parks, whatever would we do without you? Your uncle and I would have to just sit and howl at the moon!"

Her spoon clattered to the formica. Uncle Miltie! He hadn't

answered her call that morning, again, and with all the excitement . . . how could she ever have forgotten him?

"About Uncle Miltie—"

He scowled. "Don't change the subject on me."

"No." She reached to lay her hand over his. "I haven't been able to reach him."

He listened, while she told how often she'd tried to call. "It's been what—only two or three days?" he pointed out sensibly.

"It's just so unlike him!"

"Of course," he said thoughtfully, "but he's on someone else's schedule now." He tapped a fingernail to the tabletop. "Maybe he lost your phone number here and left a message in Willow Bend."

"I could ask Marge to check."

"I will, as soon as I get home. I'll let you know right away."

"I'd appreciate that."

"And I'd appreciate never again having to rescue you from a mob! Ever!" Obviously, he expected her to reassure him of her future good behavior. But how could she promise a thing like that? Especially when Gillian Pomeroy was her hostess!

"I'm happy you were there today," she said, not adding that at the time Darius Plunkett had already rescued her.

"But I can't always be!"

Hmmph! She would not be patronized or bullied by him— or by anyone.

Time to change the subject.

She gestured broadly, encompassing the charming interior of the Mercantile. "Isn't this place delightful?"

His only answer was a grunt.

"Well," Gillian announced, "it was just like the old days! They held me for questioning!"

"Oh, Gram!" Lacey's eyes welled with sympathetic tears.

"No, dear, it's a good thing, or at least it could be. The publicity, you know." She patted Lacey's arm. "Gracie's newspaper editor friend was there—had we told you?"

"Mr. Gravino." Lacey added, "He's nice."

"And a thoughtful reporter. He'll give us fair coverage, I know." She sighed. "It's just so important, dear, that we save that park."

"And the stadium." Kelly spoke from the sink, where she was filling the tea kettle. "That group of alumni will undoubtedly tear down the town if they lose it!"

"You'd think it was the Colosseum." Gillian reached to lift Gooseberry. He curled into her lap, apparently content.

Gracie was grateful she'd left him at the house that day. Just thinking about his furry body mangled by foolishly stampeding humanity enraged her.

Thank You, Lord, she began, *that no one was hurt today—at least not seriously.*

A few people in the crowd had gone to the hospital for

stitches, and one former football player had broken his foot when he kicked a fence-post. But matters could have been much, much worse. Gracie explored the bump on her head and found it now somewhat smaller, even less tender to the touch.

"We don't really need any more shops, do we, Gram? Isn't that what you're saying?"

Uncharacteristically, Gillian hesitated. "Just now, honey, I'm saying we need to get this meal up and running. There's something about a near-death experience that makes a body hungry, don't you agree?"

"You've reached the answering machine of Clint Whitley," the now-familiar message intoned, "for all the good it's done you." Gracie tapped her foot as the message droned on. "The trout are running, for one thing. For another, I can't abide these contraptions. So get a rod and bait and join me, if you want— but don't bother to leave a message. I don't care to hear it."

She waited for the tone and said briskly, "You may not care to hear it, Mr. Clint Whitley, but I'm leaving a message, anyway. You have my uncle there—wherever you are, whatever you're doing—and I need to know that he's all right. So—"

"Hello?"

Gracie gasped. Whatever she had expected, it wasn't this sweet, quavery voice.

"Hello? Are you still there?"

Gracie stammered an affirmative.

"This is Susie Ehrler, Mr. Whitley's neighbor. I feed his cats when he's away."

If he had cats, he couldn't be all bad.

Susie laughed. "I just hate his message, though I guess I've heard worse. He wants to discourage telemarketers. Now, you sound worried, dear. How can I help?"

When Gracie had explained her dilemma, Susie said, "Well, I can't be certain, of course, but he often does go fishing. And there was another gentleman with Clint when he left me the key. He had a walker, I think—the other man, I mean. At least I saw something metal in the back."

"That would be Uncle—er—George. But you don't have any idea where they went?"

Susie laughed. "With Clint, it could be anywhere from Tampa to Tenafly! I just feed the cats until I see his beat-up old green pickup back in the drive! Sometimes it's just a day, sometimes a week or two. When the cats run out of food, I buy more and leave the receipt on his counter. The cats don't mind, and it gives me something to break up my days."

"But I thought he was scheduled for some minor surgery."

Susie laughed again. "Well, I don't know about that. He's a character, Clint is. A nice man, but—did your uncle ever tell you he has a metal plate in his head? Clint, that is. From

World War II. It was a close thing, but—besides setting off alarms at airports, the only way you'd know is that once in a while—"

She paused.

"There's nothing to worry about, dear. Your uncle's safe enough with Clint."

This wasn't precisely what Gracie had hoped to hear—but at least it was something. She thanked Susie extravagantly, left Gillian's number, "just in case," and returned to the kitchen, where everyone looked up expectantly.

She rubbed at the lump on her head. "At least I got to talk to a real person instead of just that awful message." She sniffed. "*Mmm.* Smells wonderful. I could eat a horse, I think."

Deke, who'd just arrived, snapped his fingers. "You should have told us earlier! I passed a pony farm on my way here."

"Deke!" wailed Lacey. "Mrs. Parks didn't mean it!"

They were having dessert—a coconut pie from the local bakery—around the kitchen table, when they heard a crash followed by the sound of running feet.

"What—" Kelly, white-faced, was the first to her feet.

When the others joined her in the Iris Room, she held a fragment of purple glass. "Oh, Deke," she cried. "Your lovely window! If they had to break something—why that?"

He took the fragment from her, laid it aside and gathered

her in his arms. "It's fixable, honey. Just be glad we weren't at this table."

Gracie bent to pick up the chunk of concrete that had done the damage.

Gillian crouched beside her to gather a few colorful shards of glass. "The coward's special delivery method," she said scornfully.

A message was scrawled on the concrete itself in heavy black letters: STOP! OR ELSE!

"Stop what, Gram?" Lacey's eyes were wide and worried. "Your protests?" She held Gooseberry in her arms—too tightly, Gracie suspected, since his eyes were concerned, as well. She reached to loosen the girl's grip on the pumpkin-colored fur.

Gillian said softly, "Please don't worry, dear. This is merely the price one frequently pays for taking a stand."

"You mean, for trying to save the park?"

"If it wasn't that, I imagine it would be something else."

"Gram . . . it's just . . . I don't want you in danger!"

"Oh, sweetie, I've been in it before. And look at me! Not a scratch! Only wrinkles, and God put those there."

Later, in Gracie's room, Lacey fretted, "Gram enjoys the risks she takes! That's what Aunt Kelly says, anyway."

Gracie turned back the covers on her bed. "Well, worry never makes things better." She patted the bed for Lacey to sit beside her.

"I already pray a lot." Lacey nestled in the curve of Gracie's arm. "God must be tired of listening. And He must wonder why Gram doesn't . . . act like other grandmothers."

Gracie chuckled. "God never gets tired of listening to His children. That's us. Would you really want your grandmother to be any different?"

Lacey considered a moment and answered softly, "I like her the way she is." Then she finished in a whisper, "But I want her safe."

Gracie worked hard to stifle a yawn. She failed. "*Ohhh!*" she said.

Lacey giggled. "It's okay. I'm pretty sleepy myself."

Gracie smiled. "Tomorrow morning, if you like, you can join me on my prayer-walk."

"But—you'll pray tonight, too, won't you?" Lacey hesitated in the doorway, her fingertips polishing the doorknob. "About Gram—and everything?"

"Of course, my dear."

"And don't forget, I'm doing a solo in church tomorrow."

"I'm looking forward to that," Gracie assured her. "It's been a long time since I heard your voice. But I'll always remember the first time I did."

"Mrs. Parks, you're the greatest! Good night." Lacey began to walk softly out of the room, then decided to come back to give Gooseberry a good-night hug.

After she'd said her prayers, Gracie lay staring at the

ceiling stars. But thoughts of Uncle Miltie kept crowding into her mind. "Where are you?" she murmured.

She sensed no answer. And if the monkeys knew, they weren't telling.

O N THE SURFACE, Dogwood Avenue United Church was everything that Eternal Hope was not. Its marble steps, carved teakwood doors, and walls made of stone and glass conveyed an impression of architectural grandeur.

Inside, Gracie paused to gaze at the Tiffany-style windows, the crystal chandeliers, and the polished oak pews padded with crimson velvet. Above the altar, an immense round window of faceted lead crystal opened to the sky.

Spiral staircases—one short, one longer—led to suspended spherical structures—balconies, Gracie supposed you'd call them. The lower, broader one was set with curved rows of black metal folding chairs. A brass music stand—as well as its proximity to the organ—indicated that this was the choir loft.

Lacey said, "At Christmas, that's where the angels go!" They had arrived early, and Lacey was showing Gracie around.

Gracie smiled. "I know an angel who's singing here today."

Giggling, Lacey tugged Gracie toward the choir room door. "Why don't you sing with us? I'd like that so much!"

Gracie shook her head. "I haven't practiced, dear."

"The choir's doing just one song today, and it's not hard."

"Maybe during the week, if the catering's going well, I'll go to practice with you. And then next Sunday I could join you—that is, if it's all right with your director. How would that be?"

Once Lacey was gone, Gracie selected a seat in one of the front pews. She looked around her. Nodding at a couple who were settling themselves across the aisle, she couldn't help thanking the Lord for the graceful and blessed simplicity of Eternal Hope. She found it hard to picture Pastor Paul in such an ornate setting.

The very thought made her smile. Pastor Paul Meyer didn't even own a clerical collar or robe—and when one couple brought him a beautifully embroidered stole from the Holy Land, he promptly bought a glass display case for it. Pastor Paul just didn't have that self-glorifying impulse; rather, he constantly reminded worshipers at Eternal Hope that he—like the apostle Paul—was "chief among sinners," and that only One was pure and sinless and worthy of worship.

Lord, I praise You that when You came to earth You became one with us. Through Your humility, we learn humility. Through Your compassion, we learn love for others. Gracie sighed.

With the first phrases of the organ prelude, she closed with a flurry of special prayers—for Pastor Paul and the congregants at Eternal Hope, for Uncle Miltie—*oh, yes, Lord, especially for Uncle Miltie*—for Lacey, her voice and others Gracie loved best, ending with her grandson, little Elmo.

The Processional had begun.

Lacey took her place in the choir loft, looked out toward Gracie and sent a small wave.

She looks so small there, Lord, and so vulnerable. But she loves You, and she loves using her voice—Your gift to her—in Your praise.

She felt a rustling movement. Gracie made room beside her for Gillian, followed by Kelly and Deke.

In the choir loft, Lacey looked beatific.

"She's definitely special," Deke whispered, with as much pride, Gracie thought, as though they were tied by flesh and blood.

The choir sang a short call to worship, and everyone stood.

Here we go, Lord. Much as I miss Eternal Hope, You're here, and that's the important thing.

Gracie didn't need to consult the bulletin to know when it was nearly time for Lacey's solo. The entire congregation—young and old, formally dressed or more casually garbed, everyone seated in the large sanctuary—grew still with expectation.

And, just as Gracie remembered, Lacey sang like an exalted creature—the accompanist muting the organ to allow her voice to soar unfettered.

How appropriate the lyrics were.

And yet—perhaps—appropriate for any day!

> *How is it, Lord,*
> *That even though*
> *You monitor the breeze's flow,*
> *You guarantee the eaglet's flight*
> *And tell the sun to dim for night.*
> *How is it, then,*
> *With this to do,*
> *You listen when I speak to You?*
>
> *How is it, Lord,*
> *That though You guide*
> *Each rivulet and ocean tide,*
> *Each waterfall, migrating herds*
> *and rising, soaring flocks of birds.*
> *How is it, then,*
> *With this to do,*
> *You have the Will to lead me, too?*
>
> *You govern all the galaxies,*
> *Yet when I fall upon my knees*
> *I feel Your love affixed on me.*
> *Oh, tell me, Lord, how can this be?*

Lunch was Chinese takeout, complete with fortune cookies. To match the meal, Gillian set the table with colorful paper umbrellas, pointed Chinese hats and chopsticks. They all tried using the chopsticks, but only Gillian and Deke made it through more than a few tiny bites without resorting to flatware. Back in Willow Bend, at Celestial City, Gracie had once taken a lesson in chopstick use from Lum Chu, the owner. But only once, and a fork remained her preferred implement.

"I could do it," Lacey said, "if we had bigger rice." She speared a thick strip of green pepper as proof. "What does your fortune say, Mrs. Parks?"

Gracie's read, "Do not be misled by that which glitters only when observed." She looked around at her tablemates for enlightenment.

Kelly said slowly, "I think it must refer to people, Gracie. Like people who act one way to your face, and behind your back—well, you know."

Gracie studied the slim paper. "*Hmm.* I think I'll have to study it a bit more, but you may be right."

Deke teased, "Confucius say, 'Proverb not proverb if meaning is clear.'"

Gooseberry chose the moment of their laughter to ease himself out from under the table. He stood by the door, looking impatiently at his mistress.

Gracie laughed. "Woman who lets cat boss her around deserves what she gets."

~

Gooseberry once again led the way as Lacey and Gracie set off at a good pace in the direction of Dogwood Park.

Lacey giggled. "Don't you think his tail is like an orange pole? Maybe we should get Gooseberry a protest sign, like MORE DOG-FREE STREETS!"

Gracie reminded her, "He's too stubborn. He'd lower that old tail of his and sit down until we took the sign off. Whatever Gooseberry may think of dogs—and some of his best friends are, you know—he's pretty apolitical. Not like your grandmother!"

Gooseberry half-turned, as if he knew he was being discussed, and meowed a hurry-up command.

For a time they walked quietly. Gracie breathed in the rich smell of damp earth, the intoxicating fragrances of lilacs and hyacinth. Soon, they began to hum in harmony. In the middle of "Amazing Grace," Lacey broke off and said, "I'm still worried about Gram. Did you notice Deke was already working on the broken iris glass?"

"Yes, I did. And I think he's a talented young man."

"Better than that, he's nice!"

"That he is!"

A robin scolded as they inadvertently invaded its space. When they refused to hurry or to apologize, the bird swooped away, chirping disapproval.

"Like Gram, when somebody—"

"—ruffles her feathers?" Gracie finished. They both laughed.

"There's a hiking path along a stream." Lacey skipped ahead. "I like the stepping stones."

Gooseberry, at first reluctant to follow, soon acted as though it had been his idea all along.

As they ducked beneath low-hanging apple branches, Gracie heard the unmistakable murmur of water.

"Almost there—" Lacey broke off with a gasp. "Oh, Gracie, look! "

The phantom artist had been there before them, transforming each large stone into a vibrant floral abstract. They were beautiful.

"It can be summer even in winter!" Lacey exulted. "Oh, aren't they wonderful?" Skipping from stone to stone, she admired each one in turn.

Gracie's imagination sped with the running child. Here was the work of a truly inspired artist—or visionary. It should have looked wrong—to paint a landscape, literally—but, somehow, the work done on the stepping stones seemed natural. Extraordinary, but there was no denying that here was a lily that had been gilded successfully.

"You don't think it'll wash off—like the hair dye?" Lacey bent down to rub a corner of one stone. "Oh! It doesn't! I can come back and enjoy it again and again!"

Gracie considered the variety of colorful pranks being

perpetrated in Mason City—from the statue to the women's tresses. And now these stones!

Was it all connected, somehow, to the breaking of that beautifully colored glass, creation of a rival talent? Maybe the threats weren't about Gillian and her causes at all, but rather about Kelly's husband-to-be and his artistic ability. Yet it seemed incomprehensible that the creator of such beauty could destroy another's art.

"Mrs. Parks, what are you thinking? Watch me now!" Lacey commanded. Gracie instantly left off her musing to do as she was told.

Returning, they found Gillian, Kelly and Deke reading the Sunday paper. A headline, SHAME ON YOU, MASON CITY! spanned the front page. The actual melee at Dogwood Park was captured in a double-page photo spread inside. What had seemed frightening at the time now looked more comic—and certainly undignified.

"But if you think this is bad," Gillian told Gracie, "just turn to the editorial page. We all come across as foolish rabble-rousers."

"But this isn't Mr. Gravino's paper, Gram."

"You're right, honey, don't worry. Rocky—Mr. Gravino— may not always agree with me, still he ordinarily knows how to be fair-minded."

Gracie decided not to say anything. Rocky's stances sometimes tested her definition of fair-mindedness, even if he was always an impeccable reporter. Small-town papers, she thought to herself, were usually reflections of the editor's crochets, and Rocco Gravino's was no exception to this rule.

"Deke," Kelly suggested, "would you mind seeing if the store has any *Gazettes* yet?"

"Want to go with me, peanut?"

Gracie watched him fondly tousle Lacey's hair.

Lacey hesitated. "If you don't mind, I think I'll just stay here and worry with Gram."

Deke grinned. "Couldn't you worry just as well with me?"

She sighed. "You're not that great at worrying." She hugged him. "But that's okay. We like you just the way you are."

Gillian was uncharacteristically quiet as she and Gracie sat in the kitchen. Lacey and Gooseberry, curled together in an overstuffed chair, were sharing graham crackers dipped in milk. Kelly had remembered something she needed to drop off at the house of a friend.

"It's an unhappy day," Gillian sighed, "when we—as Bobby Burns wrote—'see ourselves as others see us.' It doesn't really matter what any other coverage might convey. The truth is," she tapped the photo spread, "this is the way it really was. Pictures don't lie."

"Maybe not," Gracie said, "but cameras don't have minds of their own. And photos in newspapers are selected for impact. There's always some guiding intelligence at work when it comes to the images put before us."

"Gram. . ." Lacey's voice was thick with milk and crumbs. Gooseberry was attempting to lick her face.

"It's fine, honey."

"But I don't like it when you seem unhappy."

"Lacey dear, I'm just taking advantage of an opportunity to have a good long look at myself. That was a pretty messy event the other day, and I must take some of the responsibility."

Lacey nodded, but worry still shadowed her little face.

Gillian's expression softened. "Now, don't you worry! Maybe Gooseberry would like to go out? This cat must be part dog, the way he hankers for action."

Gracie chuckled in agreement. Lacey put her furry companion down on the floor, then stood up herself. "Come on, boy," she coaxed him, and they headed out of the room. The last thing Gracie saw was a twitch of a fluffy tail; the last thing she heard was a pleased *meowww*.

Gracie turned back to her hostess. "What you've been doing is important! Without people like you, there wouldn't be a tree standing anywhere or a blade of grass not covered by concrete."

Gillian looked thoughtful. "There has to be a way to do this that won't shred what's left of Mason City's good opinion of itself!"

Suddenly a knock rattled the front door.

"I'll go," said Gracie, and as she approached, she caught the scent of spice.

"WE HAVE COME," Professor Darius Plunkett announced, "to take you on a field trip."

Deke, entering behind him, carried copies of the *Mason County Gazette*, but he laid them aside, still folded.

Making a mock bow, he extended both arms, elbows akimbo. "Miladies, if you will. I've been privileged to share a vision that I thought might intrigue you as much as it does me. Running into Professor Plunkett here was an act of the most serendipitous sort. I will say . . . no more. . . ."

"What on earth—" Gillian began. Then she accepted his one arm, Gracie the other.

Ushering them as far as the curb, Deke moved aside easels, toolboxes, canvas bags and gallon cans to make room in his van for the four of them.

Gillian observed, "You might consider a little housecleaning before this overloaded chariot goes on a honeymoon." She and

Gracie squeezed into the center section and belted in. The professor took the front passenger seat, and Deke started the engine. After only a short drive, Deke pulled to the curb and parked.

Gracie remembered these rundown buildings and broken sidewalks. They heard a woman yelling at some children from an open window, "Now you keep out of my flowers, you hear?"

Gracie searched for the flower bed referred to, but saw only a sagging windowbox, filled with brown, wilting petunias. Her fingers fairly itched to remove the twisted dead blossoms, then start clearing weeds and refuse from around an old wooden park bench slumped on rusted wrought-iron supports.

Darius Plunkett half-turned in his seat. "Now what I want you to do," he said quietly, "is concentrate. Not on the disrepair but on the architecture, the lines of the buildings, the elegant decorative touches that speak of other eras."

It was a block where each dwelling was ramshackle yet offered evidence, however faint, of better days.

"Now," Professor Plunkett continued, his voice soothing— for all the world, Gracie thought, like a hypnotist guiding a patient's recollections—"just imagine these with some straightening, rechinking, some sanding and painting."

"And money," Gillian said sadly. "A great deal of money."

"Not as much, however, as constructing a shopping center from the foundation up."

Gillian looked at him curiously. "What are you suggesting?"

Deke offered, "Mrs. Pomeroy, these structures are sound, most of them. And a lot of them are empty. Think of putting shops on the ground floors, apartments above and some of the tenants working off their rent."

The professor stepped out of the van. "Why don't we take a short walk just to survey the possibilities?" He slid open the side door and reached a hand to steady Gracie and Gillian as they stepped down. Gillian glanced back, but Gracie shook her head.

"Careful." Deke touched Gillian's elbow. "The sidewalk's uneven here."

"Of course sidewalk repair tops the list of must-do's," Plunkett said smoothly—almost silkily, reminding Gracie of Tyrone Sanders, an uncomfortable comparison. "But that will be part of Mason City's role in the project."

As they walked on slowly, Deke explained, "I could work up some drawings, of what the street might look like with some sprucing up. We need to start talking to owners. The cooperation of all the landlords is obviously the first step. But we also need to find out what the people here need, what they'd like. What I'd love for myself, and I know some of my friends would, too, is to rent one of the renovated storefronts. For a craft shop.

"But that comes later. First we need a plan, and then we can have something to talk up at a town meeting. We have to get some excitement generated—the same as we feel now—for the idea of urban renewal here in Mason City."

"Rather than the wrecking ball," said Plunkett, "we want to get a different sort of ball rolling."

"It would solve everything, don't you see? The park would be safe, and the stadium, and we'd have a shopping center with more to offer than the boring kind we can go to in Avery or everywhere else." Deke was beaming.

And all this, just from walking out the door to buy a Sunday paper. Gracie wondered what would have happened if Gillian Pomeroy had home delivery. Her future son-in-law would never have run into Professor Darius Plunkett at just the right moment.

"This is where you come in, Mrs. Pomeroy! Your organizing tactics are just what the situation calls for. You can be the one everyone will rally behind!"

Gillian looked at Gracie.

"Uh-oh," Gracie told her, "if you don't want starving wedding guests, count me out."

"If there *is* a wedding," Gillian looked transported. Gracie could almost see the gears of her mind whirring. "How can we possibly have this van honeymoon-ready with all we have to do?"

Deke looked at her fondly. "Kelly and I'll take a bus, if we have to!"

"Soon." Darius Plunkett's murmur was a promise. "Soon

a proper playground will be here. And busy, happy people."
The conversation continued, but Gracie heard it only as the rise and fall of voices, punctuated by laughter. She was staring in a different direction.

Suddenly, her companions noticed. "What is it, Gracie?"

Wordlessly, she pointed.

"Well!" breathed Plunkett.

"Wow!" echoed Deke.

Gillian nodded to herself. "The phantom artist strikes again."

In fact, Gracie realized, it was as if someone had been listening to their conversation and sketching its very spirit.

What was illustrated on the wall was incomplete. But it made its point. It was a picture of a house: cheerful, inviting, flower-bedecked. The model for it stood nearby, dilapidated as ever, but its portrait, transforming it into a storybook cottage, promised hope.

"I rest my case," said Darius Plunkett as they all began to speak at once.

*

Waiting back on Gillian's front steps were Lacey, Gooseberry and ... Rocky Gravino. Rocky stood as the van pulled up and looked on suspiciously as Professor Plunkett helped Gracie and Gillian down.

"I don't know whether you miss Willow Bend yet or not, but Willow Bend is desolate without you."

Gracie flushed, uncertain how to reply. "I don't know, this is beginning to suit me, I think," she managed, jokingly. "I get chauffeured around and fed, and someone else even walks Gooseberry!"

"Gooseberry can stay with me as long as he likes." Lacey stroked his ears. "And Mrs. Parks, too," she added hastily.

"Seriously, Gracie," Rocky coaxed. "I mean it about all of us missing you. Why don't you take a break and come back with me for a snack at Abe's?"

"I've had lunch."

"Well, so have I. But that doesn't mean a piece of cheese-cake isn't sending up a siren call! Can't you hear it, all the way from Abe's pastry display? I think it's a baritone: *Gracie! Gracie!*" he finished in a deeper than normal voice.

"Okay, you win," she told him, laughing.

Gracie might have been missing for months rather than a few days, judging from her reception at Abe's Deli. Amy Cantrell broke off from taking an order to call, "Barb said this morning she couldn't hear a single alto note. She suggested we come kidnap you if you don't come home soon."

Abe Wasserman himself couldn't stop beaming. "My favorite customer!"

"What about me?" Rocky challenged. "I weigh more than Gracie so I obviously eat more, and since I eat most of my meals here, I should be in the running, if not the top candidate for the honor!"

"Oh, I see," Abe snapped. "You think I let the cash register determine my friendships and my favorites!"

"Either that, or you simply want me to get some of that cranberry-glow hair color and a cat to match!"

"It's Gracie's personality that counts, you old pencil pusher!"

"Boys!" admonished Gracie, holding up a hand.

Because the riot at Dogwood Park was big news, Gracie was pried for further details about the goings-on in Mason City. Looking to distract her old friends from the less dignified—and also more worrisome—aspects of her stay, Gracie tried to avoid the local political brawl angle and also the rock-throwing and threatening phone calls.

Instead, she told them about the professor and Deke's jointly and joyfully conceived idea of urban renewal.

Amy suggested, "Gracie could have a café."

Abe looked interested. "Competition? I guess I could handle it."

Gracie wished Amy hadn't mentioned food! Thoughts of all that remained to be done for Kelly's wedding crowded into her mind.

Lord, I never should have accepted Gillian's invitation—not to combine a visit with a catering job. I've seen so much and found myself responding to a wonderful vision. But I also have watched a full-scale riot and seen the shards of a wantonly destroyed beautiful window. All that, and food prep, too. "It's too much," she heard herself say aloud.

Abe looked at her fondly. "Dear Gracie, let me tell you a fable." He waited a beat for Rocky's inevitable protest.

Rocky magnanimously waved him on. "Anything to keep this wonderful, generous friend of ours from killing herself with overwork."

"I will begin, then, with an old Yiddish proverb. 'If you eat a bagel, only the hole remains in your pocket.' This applies to energy, as well, my friend." He reached to take Gracie's hand.

"At the moment, you look like such a bagel, as though you have nothing left to give—either to others or to yourself. Or," he added gently, "to God."

Gracie was startled. "I guess the truth hurts," she admitted. Abe settled back.

"There was a certain bird—it could be of any species, but we will make it a red-headed woodpecker, which seems appropriate. Do you recognize yourself already, my busy friend?"

Laughing, she wondered if this "certain bird" visited a beauty shop, periodically, to have its feathers touched up.

"This was a very determined bird, a bird who could not bear the thought that anyone might hunger. All day long, she pecked and hammered at her home tree, transporting grubs to her own hungry brood. But when they were satisfied and slumbering in the nest, she did not slow her acquisition of food. And more food. And more food.

"She carried grubs to the baby woodpeckers next door, whose own parents were already busy gathering, and then to a nest of robins. Then on to some bluebirds, the meadowlarks, even the crows, whose beaks are always open wide, and whose hungers are never appeased. As time went on—as the other birds saw what was happening—they themselves worked less and less, leaving more of the feeding of their families to this one red-headed woodpecker.

"Gradually, it became more and more difficult to gather grubs and bugs from her own tree, which was now lightning-struck and dying. But when Red approached the other trees, to check their stores of food, the very parents whom she had been helping chased her away. It was fine for her to feed their children; however, if she dug into their trees, there might not be enough for them. If Red was foolish enough to try to feed the world, why should they go out of their way to help her?

"And so she pecked and carried, pecked and carried, her wings flapping with decreased energy, her body weakened by lack of the food that she continued to turn over to others. And then one day. . . ." He took a long, slow sip of iced tea. His eyes sparkled over the rim of the glass.

"Oh, no!" Rocky groaned. "Not another one of your stories without an end!"

"Actually," Abe set his glass down carefully, "there are several possible endings. The choice is Red's alone."

Gracie shifted beneath his steady gaze.

"One day, just before winter, when a chill wind blew and the grubs buried deeper and deeper for warmth, Red pecked once too often. The weakened tree groaned and swayed. . . and then, with a sigh, fell to the ground with a thundering clap that shuddered the earth. Fortunately, Red's brood had grown and flown long before, or they would certainly have perished."

Amy wondered, "And did she—the woodpecker—escape?"

"That, too, is up to Red herself."

"Is that the end?" Amy looked at Abe. "I mean, the end of the story, not Red!"

Abe gave an inscrutable smile. "One word is all I'll say," he promised. "Ask."

"Ask for what?" Amy looked puzzled.

"Well, probably they don't have food stamps for birds," Rocky said.

But Gracie understood. She promised Abe silently, but with a smile, that she would take the hint. She would ask Marge, the Turner twins and other Willow Bend friends to help her out in Mason City, just as she always did at home.

"It's time for me to head back," she said to Rocky. "Finish your cheesecake and let's hit the road!"

14

MOVING ALMOST IMPERCEPTIBLY, so as not to waken Gooseberry, Gracie slid quietly from bed before any glimmer of morning could lighten the darkness. A nightlight in the shape of a lighthouse helped her navigate the hallway. Once she was outside, Gracie inhaled deeply.

Stretching, then bending a few times and inhaling until she could testify that even her toes inflated, she greeted the men in overalls at work on the driveway two doors down and eased into her best walking pace.

This morning, no music was required. *Just You, Lord,* she began. *We do our best talking, don't we, when our focus is without distractions.*

Somewhere, a garbage can banged, and she smiled.

Well, almost uncluttered. Her senses heightened, she caught smaller sounds: the waking movement of robins in an overhanging maple, the thin high voice of a child, a closing door, a distant siren's wail.

Shivering suddenly, she remembered all too well when an ambulance had been too late to save Elmo. *Lord, whoever is in trouble this morning, be with them.* Of course it might not be an ambulance at all, but a police car speeding somewhere. To the scene of a crime? To quell a domestic dispute before violence could erupt? The site of an an accident? In any case, prayer was in order.

Please, Lord . . . whoever, whatever, wherever . . . make Your loving, healing presence felt.

Quiet enveloped her. She could hear the soft thumping of her shoes on the pavement. Broken pavement it had become, she realized with a start. Unwittingly, she had returned to the street where Professor Plunkett and Deke had taken Gillian and her early in the afternoon the day before.

The stoops were empty. A prowling cat provided the only other movement. Gracie paused, surveying the scene. Clumps of grass pushed between segments of broken pavement. Somehow, without the presence of people, the buildings looked even more desolate than they had when she'd first seen them.

How much work it will take, Lord! How much easier to bulldoze and begin again—and yet You led Nehemiah to restore the walls of Jerusalem! Restoration must be part of Your plan, then. . . .

"You just can't stay away, can you?"

Unnoticed, a man had appeared and now matched her pace.

It was Darius Plunkett, and this morning, he again had assumed his disreputable guise, the kindly wizard in mufti.

"There's been an addition," he continued, "just down here."

She allowed herself to be guided along. Darius Plunkett stopped in front of a plate glass window on which was carefully lettered: HEAVENLY GLASS. And beneath, in smaller script: D. Brandt, Proprietor and Artisan.

Gracie marveled, "Deke's storefront!"

Darius Plunkett chuckled. "That young man lets no grass grow under his feet—nor should any of us. Come walk with me a bit. Let's chat about how this Mason City renaissance might come to pass."

A dozen protests rose to mind. She needed to begin baking. She didn't even live here, for goodness sake!

Hadn't Rocky and Abe insisted she was killing herself with overwork? She didn't have time for either surprises or fresh responsibilities.

Still, she walked with him—to the area where, only yesterday, the park bench had sagged among weeds. Now, it was cleared and raked. A stack of paving stones stood ready for laying next to an eyecatching sign that read simply RENEWAL. Even the park bench looked sturdy and sparkling with new paint.

How did this happen so quickly? Gracie wondered. *Does the phantom artist work the night shift? How can he—or she—do this with no one catching a glimpse of him . . . or her?*

"Better not sit quite yet." Plunkett touched a fingertip on the underside of a bench slat. "It's still tacky."

And, Lord, who is the artist, anyway? More and more, it looks like Deke. Otherwise, why has his shop evolved overnight from fantasy into reality?

Lord, You know the identity of this elusive artist. You are undoubtedly his inspiration. Help us to accept that when the time is right for us to know this person's identity, we will.

Darius Plunkett grinned at her.

Gracie stood in Gillian's kitchen, taking stock. The night of the rehearsal dinner was nearly upon her. The Victorian dining room was already so richly appointed that little decoration would be required—or, Gracie thought, even possible!

Marge was preparing the stuffed chicken breasts in her oven, and she'd be bringing the salad, as well. The Turner twins were providing a creamy potato bake. Gracie herself would assemble the hors d'oeuvres, the relish trays, the rolls and an assortment of fruit tarts. The coffee and other beverages were being taken care of by a neighbor of Gillian's.

Unexpectedly, Uncle Miltie came to mind. Gracie had decided to give a temporary rest to her fears for his well-being. She was an independent grown-up, and so was he—even if they so often depended on one another.

But now, sinking into a chair, and thanking the Lord for

the generous help of her wonderful friends, she also prayed for her equally wonderful uncle's safety and safe return.

"Mrs. Parks! You're sitting so still!" Lacey's voice rose in concern.

Gracie looked up. "Just talking to God, dear."

"Does He always hear you?"

"*Mmm?*"

"When you talk to Him."

Gracie smiled. "He's my best friend."

Lacey leaned toward her from where she had perched on a stool. "Most people I know just talk to God when they're in trouble—you know, when they need His help. I don't think I'd like a friend like that. I'd feel . . . used."

"You have a very wise head on those little shoulders."

"Right now, my wise idea is to ask if I can help you with anything."

"That you can, my dear. Here are some apples that are just calling out to be peeled!"

They talked little as they worked. Gracie found herself enjoying the rhythmic *chop-chop-chop* and the swishing sound of sifting dry ingredients. How she loved the scrapes, clicks and whirs that were the music of a day spent baking!

Putting aside a long ribbon of peel, Lacey said, "I guess you saw Deke's shop. And the pretty bench and everything."

"I did indeed."

"Pretty neat, huh? Even if it's all still a mystery!"

Gracie closed her eyes briefly. With so much work still to do, mysteries were the last thing she needed. But it was true, more than she could explain was happening in this little Indiana town, just as it sometimes did in Willow Bend.

"Okay, Mrs. Parks?" Lacey was watching her. "You went away from me! Come back!"

"You're right, but I'm all ears now," Gracie assured her.

"And you still haven't heard the mushy song I have to sing." Lacey sighed. "It's a good thing I love them so much!"

"You mean your aunt and Deke—they wrote it?"

Lacey made a face. "The words are . . . like when there's way too much sugar in something. And chocolate syrup . . . and marshmallows . . . and a barrelful of whipped cream!"

Gracie laughed. "Sounds pretty indigestible, but if they like it, then that's all that matters. Besides, I've seen you downing all that, and then some, at the Mercantile!"

"Honest! Just let me sing it for you, Gracie! You'll see what I mean!"

She began, her voice gaining confidence as she progressed.

> *You are the sun that gilds my day,*
> *the star that sparks my night,*
> *the buttercup that dots my lawn*
> *the dearest thing I look upon*
> *is you, and only you.*

The child's voice was so pure, so sweet, so lilting that

Gracie would have enjoyed listening to her sing a railway timetable. But this was poetry that had sprung from the combined hearts of two people who knew the riches they had found in one another.

She laid aside her mixing spoon, to better listen.

You are the wave that carries me,
the breeze that cools my face,
a clear, refreshing shower
that brings my world to flower
is you, and only you.

You are the snowflake on my nose,
the touch and scent of home,
medley of bees and birds and voice—
all that insists my soul rejoice
is you, and only you.

I pledge to you my prayers, my life,
all that I am and will become—
daily I praise my Lord above,
Who grants to me this lifetime love
that's you, and only you.

The song died away, Lacey fidgeted and Gracie found herself incapable of speech.

"Didn't I tell you?"

"No."

"But I said—"

"What you said was that the song was. . . ." She searched for Lacey's exact wording. "But it isn't, dear. It's beautiful. And when you get older and find the person with whom you want to share your life, you'll realize just how splendid it is."

"Well, I do like Deke, and I love my aunt!"

Gracie caught her in a hug. "Just sing it from your heart, dear Lacey. There won't be a dry eye in the church. I guarantee it."

"So where's the next bowl of apples?"

"Right here," Gracie replied.

"I'm glad I can help you."

"You always do," Gracie assured her, "especially when you sing."

15

A SYMPHONY OF SPICES and herbs pleasantly perfumed Gillian's kitchen. When the phone rang, Kelly answered it.

"Gracie," she called, "it's for you." As she handed her the phone she murmured, "At least I think so. It's terribly garbled."

It was indeed. Thrillingly, it was Uncle Miltie's voice—but what was he saying? The few words Gracie did glean from the crackling static offered no reassurance: fish, heart, died, prayers and CPR.

"Uncle Miltie," she tried to interject more than once, "I can't understand, dear. The connection's impossible. Could you hang up and try again?"

But the line had gone dead.

"Thank goodness he's alive!" Gillian said, when Gracie returned to the kitchen. "You must be so relieved!"

Gracie was. And she wasn't. He was alive, and aware that she might be wondering about his welfare, but what about the reference to CPR? And heart? And death? She shuddered. Prayers were certainly called for.

But fish?

Anyway, where, exactly, was he? How could she reach him if she needed to? It was heartening that he had called her, but had he remembered the number? Or had Susie Ehrler given it to him?

And what about that surgery of Clint's? Maybe he'd been alluding to that? Maybe only women could be relied upon for straight answers. Should she try to contact Susie?

It should never have come to this—and wouldn't have, if she'd been the niece she thought she was. She should have discouraged him from going. She should call Clint's number right away. She should demand that Uncle Miltie come home immediately. But she wasn't at home, either, was she?

I must remember that when I asked him to come live with me, Lord, it wasn't to shut him into a cage and make him dependent. He's not a child, to be condescended to, or coddled, or controlled— forced to do what I decide is best for him. But I do so ask that You keep him safe. Please bring him back to me unharmed!

"Uncle Miltie," Gracie suddenly said out loud, "I guess the joke's on me. You've grown up and left the nest empty."

"*Huh?*" said Lacey. "Nest?"

🌿

"Mrs. Parks is coming to choir practice later," Lacey boasted. "She promised."

Gracie had forgotten. And yes, she had promised. But the wedding was the next afternoon!

Could she disappoint Lacey? But might it also, perhaps, be a way of dispelling some of her tension? In singing Gracie found a joy that no other task—not even her beloved kitchen chores—could fully equal. She protested weakly, "Could I just finish the cleanup? Load the dishwasher, at least?"

"Nonsense," Gillian said. "Deke will do it."

She and Kelly collapsed in laughter, but Deke, grabbing an apron, teased, "It won't be the last time, I'll bet."

Gracie hesitated. There wasn't much left to do, really. Her Willow Bend cohorts had taken their own serving dishes home.

Lacey was doing a nervous little dance. "Hurry, Mrs. Parks!"

Straightening her shoulders, Gracie followed.

Arriving at Dogwood Avenue United with Lacey, Gracie thought again how much less warm and welcoming it seemed than Eternal Hope. The Lord was there, she knew, and the people weren't actually standoffish. Perhaps the lack was more hers than theirs. She'd have to think about that.

It's interesting, too, she thought, the differences among choir leaders—and choir members, for that matter. But perhaps even more startling are the similarities.

The Dogwood United director was a man, with the authority of a working academic in his demeanor. Noel Talbot had made music his entire life, and his reward was a tenured job at nearby Jefferson College. Yet his passion for music and his striving for perfection were identical to Barb's, whose directing was primarily self-taught.

"Welcome," Noel Talbot said. The fact that, in his choir, altos were in short supply meant his greeting undoubtedly was sincere. At precisely 7:30 P.M., he rapped his podium with his baton.

As with Barb Jennings, this choir director had a strong allegiance to promptness.

Early on the morning of the wedding, when Gracie and Gooseberry returned from their prayer-walk, they found Gillian sitting with a mug of steaming tea.

"How could you possibly go for a walk, this day of all days!" Her tone indicated amazement rather than disapproval. "I'd find it too distracting!"

"It's just the opposite for me." Gracie reached out to stroke Gooseberry. "A morning prayer-walk seems to be the only way I can really get myself to focus."

Gillian sighed. "I guess it's too late to postpone the wedding for a day or two, until the mother of the bride pulls herself together?"

Gracie patted Gillian's shoulder. "You'll be fine. You're not the one who's supposed to be nervous, anyway. And you'll have Deke's mother to keep you company!"

"Tell my tummy butterflies that!"

"Just remember, you're not losing a daughter—"

"I'm gaining a son. I know that, and I couldn't love Deke more if he were my own. It's just that I want everything to be perfect for Kelly—this time."

"And if it isn't? If someone misses a step in the processional —or miscues—"

"I know—in life, one can't simply press the 'rewind' button!"

Gracie reached over to cover Gillian's hand with her own. "My husband Elmo and I had a marriage that was just about perfect. But the strains and compromises were always there, too, along with the blessings. God gives us the good along with the bad, and the frustrating, too.

"Like when a husband puts off fixing the leaky faucet, or won't drop his socks in the laundry, or reads the paper at the table, or never notices the little things a wife does to make dinner special. Can we agree that Deke will never demonstrate any of these particular flaws?"

"Of course."

"Still, he may display one or two others. And I'll wager that Kelly's not perfect, either." She stood briskly. "And who could stand to be around them if they were? Let's get to work! We have a wedding to produce!"

Yawning, Kelly entered. She made slowly for the stove,

where the teakettle breathed silent puffs of steam. "Mom, I'm off to the beauty shop." She raised a hand to forestall argument. "Even you went back and got your style freshened up at Harriet's, so don't try to pretend you didn't. I could tell."

Gillian made another attempt to interrupt, but again, Kelly cut her off.

"Rather than be late for my wedding and give Deke a chance to escape, I'm perfectly willing to risk hair the color of some lurid sunset!" She carried her mug to the table.

"And, remember, no permanent damage occurred. I guess they've checked all the usual suspects." She shrugged. "I'm not even sure who those would be! But it's my wedding day, and I know God is watching over me and all bottles of questionable hair color, too."

Carrying in the final tray to the Dogwood United kitchen, Gracie found her Willow Bend crew already assembled. Marge stretched white plastic covering over a long serving table while the Turner twins tied ruffled pale blue aprons over identical embroidered skirt and sweater sets.

Lacey, helping with the place settings, positively vibrated with excitement. Every few seconds, she executed an impromptu dance step, or hummed a snatch of the wedding march.

"Oh, I can't *wait*! I just can't *wait*! I just can't *wait*!" she kept repeating. Eventually, she abandoned her efforts at helping.

"Mrs. Parks," she called out, "you'll never guess what Deke's giving Aunt Kelly! Besides a ring, I mean. He's made her a—"

She looked in all directions, as though anticipating spies, then whispered, "It's stained glass!"

This didn't require any of my detective skills, Gracie thought.

"It's Aunt Kelly and me, watching swans, and it's as big as us!" She pointed. "It's over there!"

"That big one? That looks like a tabletop?"

Lacey giggled. "Won't she be surprised? And all she's giving him is cufflinks."

She's wrong, Lord, Gracie confided. *Kelly is giving him much, much more than cufflinks. She's giving him a heart that's been bitterly wounded, but healed, and all the stronger for that. She's giving Deke her life, as well as her love . . . and she's giving him this dear child, whose care she has made her own.*

She said none of this aloud—only hugged Lacey tightly before returning to work.

Gracie and her crew, taking a break, slipped into the sanctuary to see the floral arrangements. Gracie might formerly have argued that simplicity could not be sumptuous. Now she saw that that seeming contradiction could be achieved. Deke's family, she knew, had conferred via telephone, to take care of this aspect of the festivities. Only his mother was to be there, but the Dogwood United ladies, in conjunction with Mason City's fanciest florist, had done Mrs. Brandt proud.

Branched brass candelabra, each holding a forest of slender ivory tapers, were placed around the church. Two massive sprays of calla lilies in four-foot tall brass vases flanked the marble altar. Encircling the huge window above was a wreath made of gold ribbon loosely braided among large magnolias, a design repeated at the entrance to each pew.

The arrival of the organist reminded Gracie and her friends of their duties elsewhere. But throughout the ceremony, while they made last-minute preparations in the kitchen, Gracie pictured the tapers lit, and casting their warm glow on the magnolias.

Fortunately, the sound system piped the ceremony to where the women worked in efficient harmony. Gracie paused when Lacey sang, and Marge dabbed at her eyes. "That was *so* spectacular. Like a movie!"

"Beauti—," Tyne began, as Tish finished, "—ful."

Marge went on, "The tune seemed vaguely familiar, but I didn't recognize the words."

Gracie said, "The bride and groom wrote them. Of course, even if she sang them so gloriously, Lacey thought they were too . . . mushy."

Her friends all laughed. "She's too young to have been—"

"—in love! She'll change—"

"—her mind!"

"My sentiments exactly!" Gracie exclaimed, her eyes brightly moist.

Lacey was the first to come downstairs when the organist had scarcely begun the post-ceremony music. Swirling and turning, so that her skirt flared about her, she danced over to Gracie. Kelly's bouquet, filling her arms, combined calla lilies, gardenias, magnolias and tendrils of tiny-leafed ivy. "Aunt Kelly was afraid I might not catch it—so she just gave it to me!

"And you were right, Mrs. Parks. Everybody cried!"

"Your song was a splendid success. We heard it!"

"And—" Lacey looked shyly at Gracie. "When I watched them—Aunt Kelly and Deke—while I was singing . . . you were right, the words didn't sound silly, anymore."

It was over. Kelly and Deke were gone, their suitcases thrown blithely into the still-cluttered van, crepe paper fluttering from the antenna and a trail of aluminum cans bouncing and banging down the street. Deke's mother had hugged poor Lacey until she had almost no breath left. Then she departed, though not before heaping Gracie with praise. And hugging her, too, for good measure.

By dinnertime, definitely wilted, Gillian, Gracie and Lacey had settled in the Pomeroy kitchen to feast on leftovers. Lacey had saved nearly a dozen precious chocolate-covered strawberries and was making each one last as long as possible.

The Willow Bend crew had long ago left for home.

The tired trio was unprepared for a brisk knock at the door. The prospect of visitors was almost beyond energy.

When Gillian groaned, dropping her head to the tabletop, Gracie assumed the duty of doorperson. Once again, standing before her was Darius Plunkett.

Following her to the kitchen, the professor noted, "You ladies look like an ad for vitamin deficiency."

Gracie sank into her seat. "The problem is wedding-itis."

He snapped his fingers. "How thoughtless! I forgot it was today. I just wanted to share my excitement—"

Gillian looked up. Despite her weary expression, she looked attractive in her stylish mother-of-the-bride dress.

Darius Plunkett definitely noticed. He seemed to take in her elegant hairdo, as well.

"Can I get you some coffee?" Gracie asked. "Tea?"

"Oh, yes, forgive me." Gillian indicated a chair, and pushed the tray of leftover canapés toward him. "Please have one. Have many!"

"Coffee then, please, Mrs. Parks. Black."

As Gracie poured the coffee, Plunkett said drily, "Quite a different social dynamic from a protest march."

Gillian smiled. "You get to wear more comfortable clothes and less make-up at a demonstration."

"But this makes for a very nice change," he replied. And

Gillian, looking a little less tired when she blushed, smiled again.

They make a handsome couple, Gracie thought suddenly, startled by the revelation.

Lacey had momentarily stopped her slow licking of the chocolate from a strawberry. Her glance moved wonderingly from her grandmother to Plunkett. "What excitement?" she asked. Everyone looked in her direction.

Crossing her arms, she said impatiently, "When you came in. You were talking about sharing. . . ." She took a large bite and chewed thoroughly. "Well?"

Professor Plunkett furrowed his brow.

"You've forgotten!" Lacey accused.

He seemed to be struggling for an instant, then his face cleared. "The playground!" he said. "I came to take you—all of you," he amended. "To see the latest developments."

Lacey scrambled from her chair. "We're ready!"

The strawberries, Gracie noted, were gone—all but two, which Lacey squirreled away in a silverware drawer.

16

IT WAS CERTAINLY not as dramatic as the feeding of the five thousand, but it seemed a miracle, nonetheless.

Where previously there had been rusting garbage cans and clumps of dusty weeds, now Gracie saw a play space creatively conceived and assembled.

The lines of the equipment were simple, the wooden construction practical and rugged—and Gracie suspected that even if the jungle gym, swings, teeter-totters, merry-go-round and slides had been left unpainted, the children would have been as thrilled. However, someone had gone wild with pattern and color.

The jungle gym, in shades of bright green, was far too vivid to pass as the camouflage it simulated. The seats of the smaller swings glowed hot pink and violet, and the slide was blue-and-yellow striped. It was simultaneously witty, merry and welcoming.

"No trees yet," Darius Plunkett said, "but they will come."

And now, Gracie noticed, in the fading light where only brambles had flourished before, there were newly planted shrubs—rhododendrons, forsythia, mockorange, boxwood and lilac—all small but showing great promise for the future.

"How did he do it all?" Gillian murmured. "With the wedding and everything?"

"Who?" asked Lacey.

"Deke, of course."

"He said he didn't. Or that's what he said before."

"I know," Gillian was puzzled. "But why? It's unlike him . . . to be untruthful."

Lacey corrected her grandmother. "He'd never lie, Gram! And we mostly always knew where he was. He mended your iris window, remember? And he made that beautiful, beautiful gift for Aunt Kelly."

Gillian nodded. "You're right, but who else is there, dear?"

"Even in a city as small as this one," Professor Plunkett suggested, "there must be many others with both artistic talent and a love for his or her neighbors."

Back in Gillian's kitchen, the professor allowed himself to be talked into another cup of coffee. He was murmuring approval of a miniature fruit tart when Lacey offered him a precious strawberry.

"It lasts longer if you lick it slowly," she volunteered helpfully.

"Thank you, dear girl, for your advice," he replied gravely.

Even though Gracie was accustomed to praise for her catering, she'd received more exhaustive kudos only when Rocky Gravino first sampled her peach and apricot pie.

His appetite appeased, Darius Plunkett told them that Deke and he had secured a slot at the next town council meeting, to present their vision of urban renewal as an alternative to the construction of a standard-issue new shopping center.

"You must be there, Gracie!" Gillian ordered, looking more imperious than exhausted.

"Indeed," Professor Plunkett seconded. "The more people we have in support of our alternative plan the better." He lifted a last fragment of apple tart in an appreciative salute and closed his eyes as he savored it.

Lacey gave Gracie a dark glance.

Why, Gracie realized, she's jealous of me! Not for herself, but on behalf of her grandmother. She must sense that spark of attraction lit between them and hope it will truly ignite. And my desserts and I pose a threat!

"Lacey, in fact, peeled the apples," Gracie said quickly. "And it's really Gillian who organized everything for Kelly and Deke. It was her idea I come over to lend my skills, and she kept us all in line, in addition to spearheading the park protest."

Professor Plunkett cast admiring eyes once again in Gillian's direction.

Gracie observed this as avidly as Lacey, but with a different spirit. El would have enjoyed all this, she thought, and the spectacle of that wonderful playground, above everything else.

⟡

Gooseberry was lightly snoring when Gracie, drowsing over a mystery in bed, heard the phone ring. Listening closely, she heard no evidence that Gillian had answered. She'd nearly convinced herself to ignore it—the machine would pick it up—when a sudden picture of Uncle Miltie, bruised and bandaged, intervened.

It was, after all, nearly midnight. Who called at such an hour without some compelling reason?

Not even pausing for her slippers, she scurried down the staircase. *Rrring!* How soon would the machine come on? And would whoever it was leave a message or just hang up?

Her breath caught. The more she tried to rush, the clumsier she seemed to become. Like that Pennsylvania Dutch saying: "The hurrieder I go the behinder I get." Was that it? *Rrring! Ouch!* She rammed her shin against a table edge. Or was it that anonymous pest with some new threat for Gillian, she wondered. *Rrring!*

Suddenly the recorded message kicked in: "You have reached the Pomeroy residence. I'm sorry no one—"

"Hello?" Gasping, Gracie pushed the stop button to cut short the recording.

"Gracie?"

"Herb?" She straightened. Why would Willow Bend's chief of police be calling—unless—

"Forgive me for calling so late, but—"

"You've heard something? About Uncle Miltie?"

"Well, I'm not sure." She could almost see him leaning back in his desk chair. Perhaps he'd be rubbing his forehead, as he did sometimes when perplexed. It was late for him to be in his office, she knew that for a certainty!

"Please, Herb. Whatever it is—" She swallowed hard. She had been about to say that she could handle it. But could she?

"I'm not sure if this means anything or not, but there was a fishing boat found—"

"Where, Herb?" Her voice had grown small.

"Canada. A lake one hundred and fifty miles north of the border." He hesitated. "The boat had capsized. They found two knapsacks, but no . . . no. . . ."

"Bodies," she supplied. "No bodies."

"There was evidence of a campfire not far inland. But no way to tell how old. It had been raining."

"The knapsacks?"

"No identification, just rations. No identifying marks. Could you describe his?"

She thought back to his packing, to his departure. "He didn't take one."

"Gracie?"

"*Mmm?*"

"I just can't picture him going off to Canada, can you? Where is it his friend lives? I'm probably overreacting."

"Pittsburgh. Not in, but near."

"Lake Erie would make more sense, then, right?"

"Right. But you know as well as I do that Uncle Miltie sometimes exhibits more gumption than sense."

"I think this is the equivalent of a wild goose chase. But I was sure you'd want me to notice anything that could smack of a missing Uncle Miltie. I'm really sorry to have called so late."

"I haven't had a chance, Herb, to tell you I heard from him. But the connection was so terrible, he was more likely phoning from Mars, not Canada. I couldn't understand a word he was saying, unfortunately."

She winced, knowing that wasn't totally true. She had heard *CPR*, heart, prayer and died....

HOW SELFISH I AM, LORD, she prayed as she drifted off to sleep. *Forgive me. Whether or not this was Uncle Miltie and his friend, someone's boat has capsized. Someone is missing. How many families—reading this in the newspaper or hearing it on the news—will be certain that their loved one is involved?*

She read another page from the devotional book *Daily Guideposts* and shut out the light. When she was usually so voluble, so at ease in speaking with the Lord, why were her thoughts so paralyzed?

There were a dozen petitions she might frame, but the magnitude of the fears and griefs of all mankind seemed to press against her. For every Uncle Miltie who might or might not be endangered on a fishing expedition, there were thousands of fathers, sons and uncles whose loved ones anguished over their well-being.

She drew a long breath of sadness, and moments later, the words came in a rush. *How can You bear it, Lord—this constant suffering of Your people? Forgive me when I bother You with so many unimportant things. Lord, I cannot imagine going through even a day without talking to You. And please, wherever he is, please make Uncle Miltie aware of Your presence . . . and Your love. Amen.*

At such moments, Elmo seemed very close to her, and yet indescribably unreachable. She closed her eyes and pictured the handsome, kind and intelligent face of the late Elmo Parks. He, too, loved God as she did, as a friend in every circumstance and a beacon in all darkness.

In a second, before finishing another thought, Gracie was fast asleep.

"Gracie," Lacey whispered as she and her visitor took their places in the choir loft. "Don't forget to pray for Uncle Miltie."

Gracie nodded to show she had heard.

"We give Thee but Thine own," they sang. The hymn was familiar enough that Gracie's attention could easily split in two directions. The later selection would be more difficult, but beautiful enough to warrant struggle—an intricate embellishment of "The Beatitudes."

You bless the poor,
the poor who—all but dead—
huddle in rat-infested alleyways,
with filthy rags and cardboard for a bed . . .
who wrest a scant, unhealthy sustenance
from scraps unsuitable for others—
as they themselves are judged unfit—
shielded from view of children
by their mothers,
shunned by the fortunate, well-clothed, well-fed,
while, loving Lord,
You bless the poor, embrace the poor, exalt the poor!
Garments of righteousness replace
the shreds they're wearing.
Reaching to You, they marvel at Your caring.
Your love surrounds, uplifts,
Invades their deepest griefs—
and from the world's rejections . . . grants relief.
You bless the poor
You bless the poor . . . You bless the poor!

Such a complex choice would be an unlikely part of any service at Eternal Hope. The congregation would tolerate it, and Pastor Paul might be thrilled, acknowledging with humility that it left little for his sermon to say.

But the choir itself?

That was another matter altogether. Even considering the soaring soprano obligato, Estelle would surely lead any mutiny. Marge would be nervous and Don Delano precise. Lester Twombley might remark, "The service is only an hour long—remember?" And the Turner twins chime in with, "Oh, my, this is truly—"

"—difficult, isn't it? Are you certain—"

"—we won't mess it up?"

Only Amy Cantrell and Rick Harding would welcome the challenge.

Or am I being unfair, Lord? Many times, Gracie had seen her Eternal Hope friends stretch and grow. Perhaps she should ask the director for a copy of the anthem, in order to give the singers back in Willow Bend a chance to try something new.

In the meantime, the minister was calling for prayer. Bowing her head, Gracie remembered Lacey's admonition and sent up a plea that admitted she even missed her uncle's corny jokes. *Send him back to me, Lord, and he can ask me 'Knock-Knocks' until the cows all come home. I promise I won't roll my eyes, but will laugh every time!*

Gillian sighed. "How can I thank you, Gracie? And how will we get along without you? I already miss you!"

Gracie laughed. "You seemed to be doing quite well before

I came. And—" she straightened from her packing—"you have given me a memorable two weeks!"

"Mrs. Parks," Lacey spoke softly, "you will come back, won't you?"

Before Gracie could answer, Gillian said. "Of course she will! For the town council meeting a week from tonight!"

"Oh, really—"

"There's no debate. You'll be here."

"You're just counting on my well-developed sense of curiosity." Gillian laughed.

"You can come with Mr. Gravino," Lacey interjected.

Rocky?

Why, of course Rocky would want to be there—would *need* to be there! This was news that mattered in greater Mason County!

"Well, then—"

Gillian now spoke affectionately. "We really do need you, dear friend. You bring with you an insight most of us lack. And a generous spirit that is uniquely yours, as well."

"Plus, she's such a delicious cook!" Lacey looked at them with a smile that began to droop. "Oh, everything is just perfect, isn't it? All we need is for Mr. Morgan to be safe."

18

WHO WAS IT, GRACIE WONDERED, who had written, "The best thing about leaving home is the joy of returning?"

Her surge of gladness began at the outskirts of Willow Bend. By the time she pulled in front of her own clapboard house, she was nearly weak with her pleasure in the familiar landscape.

Gooseberry obviously shared her feelings. Long before home was in sight, he had plastered himself against the passenger window, his loud meows blending anticipation and impatience.

Marge was in Gracie's kitchen, awaiting her friend's arrival. A telephone call earlier had alerted her to her best friend's estimated time of return. The two women hugged as if it had been years and not mere days since they had last seen one another.

Marge dragged Gracie out on a tour of her yard and garden. "Just look at your petunias! I've never seen them look healthier, have you? I gave them lots of TLC and a new plant food. I can let you try some, if you like."

After admiring the flowers, they returned to Gracie's kitchen.

"I even dusted. Well, not a lot, actually, but when I was watering the houseplants if I made fingerprints I wiped them away. I used your wonderful lemon spray."

"I put all your mail over here. It's divided into bills, catalogues, junk mail, and real letters." Marge preened. "Maybe I could get out of the gift shop business and become an executive assistant!"

Once they had settled with mugs of tea and buttered toast, Marge took a deep breath and asked, "Uncle Miltie?"

Gracie sighed. "Let's just continue operating on the principle that no news is good news."

Suddenly, as if on cue, a knock came at the back door. Herb Bower entered, smiling reassuringly.

"Herb—" Gracie began. His genial expression went a long way toward making her feel better.

"Those men on the capsized boat—they weren't Uncle Miltie and his pal."

Her swift relief shamed her.

"And they weren't hurt much, either," he continued. "That is, except for the flesh wound one of them received when they'd robbed a Buffalo, New York, convenience store at gunpoint."

Marge gasped.

"But, Herb, I don't think you'd be telling me this if it didn't have *something* to do with Uncle Miltie. Did he suddenly turn into a convenience-store robbing arthritic octogenarian with a walker?"

Herb smiled, then said, "No, but you're close."

Now it was Gracie's turn to gasp.

"No, no," he soothed. "Not to worry. When the two prisoners were being questioned—since I'd been making inquiries—the RCMP officers asked if they'd seen two fishermen, one of whom fitted your uncle's description."

"RCMP?" interrupted Marge.

"Royal Canadian—"

"—Mounted Police, of course!"

"The crooks remembered the walker."

"Where was he?" Gracie corrected herself, "Where were they?"

"It seems your uncle's friend had said they were headed for the remotest point they could find—somewhere where they'd have to park his truck and hike."

"Hike! Uncle Miltie with his walker!"

"It gets worse. When these guys were arrested, guess what they were driving."

Marge sank into a chair. "Clint Whitley's truck! They left them stranded!"

Herb nodded grimly. "The robbers hitched a ride with them, then waited until they were safely out of earshot, hot-wired the engine and hightailed it out of there. But when the pick-up ran out of gas, they simply went on to another vehicle that had a full tank."

"But they're sure it was Uncle Miltie?"

"The plates are registered to Clint Whitley. Pretty adventurous old fellow, you have to admit."

"So," Marge demanded, emphasizing his title, "What are you going to do, *Sheriff* Bower?"

Gracie said, "Marge, be reasonable. What can Herb do from here? Besides, I did hear Uncle Miltie's voice, that once!"

Said Herb, "I've been in close telephone contact. There's a search party out, made up of guys who know those remote spots, and where the fish are. They promised to call as soon as they learn more."

Gracie found it hard to believe what she was hearing. Her elderly uncle had taken the bus to Pittsburgh to comfort a sick friend, and next thing she knew, he was in Canada and stranded in the wilderness!

Herb added, "I left them my cell phone number."

Gracie nodded.

"In fact," he said, consulting his watch, "I'd hoped we'd hear while I'm here."

"I haven't even unpacked yet," Gracie said. "Marge ambushed me when I walked in."

Just then Herb's cell phone shrilled. As he pulled it out of its case, Gracie and Marge watched, their eyes wide. He spoke for a few minutes, then handed the phone to Gracie.

"Hello?"

"Gracie!" This time Uncle Miltie came through loud and clear.

"You're—"

"All in one piece, thank the good Lord! I suspect some heavy-duty praying. But look, dear, I have only a few seconds. All kinds of adventures to report when I get home. Can you meet us tomorrow at O'Hare? The afternoon flight from Toronto."

"Of course!"

"Okay if Clint stays with us? Just for a few days?"

"Of course. . . ."

"I knew you wouldn't mind! Oh, and don't forget to bring a wheelchair. Gotta go, dear! See you tomorrow! Love you!"

And quickly, the line was dead.

"A wheelchair!" She looked from Marge to Herb. "What on earth do you suppose he's done to himself?"

But how could they possibly know?

"Rocky, Abe . . . I'm worried."

"There's just no pleasing you," Rocky teased. He caught her elbow with careful concern. "First you fuss because you don't hear, then because you do."

"Is a wheelchair necessarily a bad thing?" Abe signaled to Amy to refill their mugs. "In the cold and damp of Canada, his arthritis may have kicked up—enough that the walker seems not enough for a long walk through a terminal. And who knows where you may find parking space? Now, if he had asked for an ambulance and gurney—"

He waved his hands expressively. "Then even our intrepid editor friend here would be frowning."

Amy looked at Gracie with affection. "It's so great to have you back! You can't know how we missed you in choir—" She shook her head for emphasis. "In fact, Willow Bend just isn't Willow Bend without you!"

Rocky caught Gracie's hand, which he patted fondly. "From what I hear, Mason City isn't the same since she went there, either. Riots, broken windows, a picketer snatched from the jaws of disaster by her old pal Gravino. And," he added, "never a word of thanks for his courage and gallantry."

Gracie refused to humor him. "He's just jealous," she told Abe and Amy, "that someone else can stir up a fuss besides him."

"Newspapermen!" Amy clucked.

"But just try getting along without us! That's how you know the world's still ticking along. Forget that TV business! It's the power of the press that matters."

"Yes, sir!" Amy made a mock salute.

"Well," said Abe. "Uncle Miltie's going to deserve a banner headline when he does finally get back home! Isn't that right, Rocky?"

"Sounds like a great story...," Rocky agreed.

"But I want to hear it from him before I read it in the paper," Gracie said.

"Maybe they can turn him into a movie-of-the-week," Rocky joked. "Mel Gibson can play me!"

Gooseberry, perhaps afraid that another journey was in the offing, failed to come when Gracie called. He considered himself well-hidden, she supposed—having no idea that his tail, flicking playfully beyond the vegetable garden fence, was like a flag.

While she could understand his reluctance, she hated being late for choir practice. After popping inside to look for a treat with which to lure him, she returned to find him truly gone.

"Oh, Gooseberry!" She searched for another fifteen minutes before leaving, hoping that by the time choir practice was finished, he'd be waiting for her. He wouldn't be contrite, she knew—she'd never expect such humility. The best her cat could muster would be forgiveness.

The choir was vocalizing as Gracie hurried into the building. But, the moment she opened the door to the sanctuary, everyone—except Estelle—stopped short. Barb, cueing them at the piano, looked around, her face glowing. "Welcome home!"

There were spatterings of applause, a few cheers, and a mass exodus from the chairs to greet her up close.

"I told you," Amy said softly. But, after several minutes, Barb briskly tapped her baton, and the business of singing the Lord's praises again took over their attention.

It's good, Lord, to be back here where I belong. Dogwood United is beautiful and a fitting tribute to Your splendor. But for someone like me, it's like putting a meat and potatoes person at a banquet with caviar and escargot. There, I'm reminded primarily of Your kingship—and that's essential—but here I feel I can also approach You as Father.

Smiling, and inhaling the familiar scents of Eternal Hope Community Church, she carried the alto section with confidence and joy.

GRACIE WAS RELIEVED when Marge offered to close her gift shop for the day and go with her along to the airport.

Her friend knew she would rather wrestle hungry tigers than cope with large airports alone. They were miracles of human ingenuity and inspired technology, but they intimidated her with their hugeness and their complexity, their echoing smorgasbord of sound, and the endless, milling sea of strangers!

I do love all of Your children, Lord. I just feel so much more at ease when they come in small groups! In these corridors, I imagine I know what a salmon feels like, plowing resolutely up a waterfall—

"They're here!" Marge shouted suddenly, and waved madly.

Gracie could scarcely contain her apprehension—and her happiness.

They were waiting by the gate indicated for Uncle Miltie's

flight. Marge had explained the circumstances to one of the customer service representatives, and they had agreed that an elderly man in a wheelchair, even one accompanied by a friend, could have his niece on hand to greet him as he came off the plane.

"Look for the wheelchair! The wheelchair!" Marge continued to point.

Obviously, Marge didn't mean the borrowed wheelchair—folded and leaning against the wall—that they had brought with them.

Gracie scanned the crowd, not an easy task with Marge jostling her and hissing in her ear, "See it? Surely you can see!"

Finally, Gracie spotted an airline steward pushing a wheelchair. "That's not Uncle Miltie!"

"You're sure?" Marge shielded her eyes with her hand. "He's about the right age—"

"But bigger, with a crewcut." She drew a deep breath. "There he is!"

"Where? Where? I can't see, Gracie. There's only that one wheelchair!"

But Uncle Miltie was coming toward them, past the gate exit, under his own steam. In fact, he was walking straighter than Gracie had seen him in a long time. And he was carrying his folded walker. At that moment he spotted them, and raised his walker in a salute. His smile seemed a yard wide.

It's true, Gracie told the Lord—as though He didn't already know from long experience with men such as David, Jonah, Moses and Nehemiah. *Give a man a challenge, and if he can rise to it, his confidence and abilities multiply.*

"Now, tell me again," Rocky said later in Gracie's kitchen, "and this time slowly enough that I get the details."

Clint Whitley watched his new friends with good humor.

And there's another surprise, Lord. Mr. Whitley's nothing like what I expected. He's just an old honey.

Uncle Miltie's old buddy had a military bearing and eyes like blue topaz, sharp and bright, with crow's feet that deepened when he laughed, which was often.

Uncle Miltie licked his ice cream spoon and began. "We wanted to get as far from civilization as our feet and my walker, which had me a bit worried, would take us. Clint assured me the path wasn't too bad, that he knew it well and that I'd scoot right along."

Clint broke in with, "I knew my buddy George could climb like a mountain goat."

"In Italy, yes. But how many decades ago was that, man?"

Rocky said, "Hate to rush you boys, but I have a deadline. Let's get back to the story. So, you drove as far as the truck could make it, said goodbye to your hitchhikers, and then set off on foot?"

"Loaded down with enough stuff to last us through Christmas." Uncle Miltie threw Clint a challenging grin.

"The potato chips were your idea."

"They're lighter than those jars of peanut butter!"

"Yeah, but hard to eat when they're reduced to powder after being carted around in a backpack!"

Rocky cleared his throat.

Gracie suggested gently, "Why don't you just get to the part about Clint's fall?"

She could have told the story herself. They had been sitting around a campfire—miles from where they'd parked Clint's truck—watching the sparks rise and fade and reliving the glory and fear of World War II. All of a sudden Clint had told Uncle Miltie he thought something they'd eaten must not have agreed with him.

"George never was much of a cook," Clint growled.

Uncle Miltie said, "This from the guy who thinks you make Swiss steak with chocolate!"

"Chocolate?" a young voice piped from the living room.

Gracie had nearly forgotten Patsy Clayton. Earlier, resting against the bar of her own small walker, she'd shown up at the front door and asked if she could visit Gooseberry for a game of jacks. She'd bounce the ball, and Gooseberry would fetch it or one of the small metal jacks. Usually, for obvious reasons, he chose the ball.

"There are some cookies I can get for you in a second, dear!" Gracie called.

"But I thought Clint was having surgery and Uncle Miltie

was coming to help out and keep you company." This came from Marge.

"*Aww*, I postponed it. Too much fun having George around to hang out with—why waste his visit?"

But even if Clint had postponed his minor surgery, his heart hadn't been aware that it was at a remote campsite. It picked that minute to go into spasm, causing Clint to clutch his chest and fall forward.

"I praise the Lord every day for that CPR class, Gracie—and for your insistence that I take it!" Uncle Miltie looked fondly at his niece.

Whenever he reached that point in the story, Clint nodded soberly. "This was the *second* time my buddy George saved my life," he said. "Once in Italy—" He never elaborated on that event; Uncle Miltie's warning look would have turned a magpie mute.

"At first," Uncle Miltie continued for his friend, "my aim was to get him to the truck. Call for help. But the farther we went—"

"I thought he'd got us lost," Clint admitted.

"And told me so!"

"Loudly and repeatedly, I'm sorry to say." Clint reached a hand to Uncle Miltie's shoulder. "Should have remembered—my buddy George has the instincts of a bloodhound."

"I even started worrying, myself, after a few hours." Uncle Miltie sighed. "I was wearing out, and no truck was in sight.

Felt like I was back on the farm, wrestling livestock. Even with him leaning on my walker, he was close to dead weight. And then on that narrow spot along the ravine—"

"I still think you pushed me, old buddy." Clint's tone belied any seriousness.

Uncle Miltie ignored him. "The place Clint said would be no problem at *all* for my walker. Easy as melting butter with a blowtorch, he said."

Clint challenged, "And you made it, didn't you?"

"No thanks to you, standing at the other end, clucking like a chicken!"

Rocky cleared his throat. "But it was at this juncture you fell, Mr. Whitley?"

"Over and over—"

"Grabbing for branches. Yipping and yelling—"

"Never knew stones grew so hard!"

"He started a little avalanche," Uncle Miltie said wonderingly. "And raised enough dust to plant a field of sweet corn!" Shaking his head, he added, "Looking back . . . it's almost funny."

Clint cleared his throat. "Not to me! The going was already bad enough, but the falling was worse. Thought I'd broke every bone in my body. And how my heart held up through it all, I'll never know!"

Rocky said, "And Uncle Miltie. . . ."

"I skittered down, calling his name. When I got there he

was still, and white—" Uncle Miltie shuddered. "I thought he was dead."

"Me, too. But when I was inconsiderate enough to still be alive, my old buddy here did more than any friend could ever ask."

They were silent, and in the interval the refrigerator's murmur seemed thunderous.

Then, clearing his throat, Uncle Miltie said, "I knew I could never make it under my own power. And yes, Gracie, I did pray—a lot!"

"Both of us did."

In her thoughts, Gracie added, *All of us did, didn't we, Lord?*

"So I made a sled with my walker and some pine boughs, so I could pull him."

"I swear he tried for thornbushes. When he couldn't find any, those prickly pine needles were the best revenge he could think of."

"I could slide him along easier, then," Uncle Miltie said. "But more than once—" His voice broke.

"We thought we were done." Clint nodded soberly. "For certain. Thought we'd caught our last fish."

"Yep. And then, when we got to the place where we knew the truck was—"

"—or had been. . . ."

"When we realized what had happened . . . well, I felt like an orange with the juice all sucked out."

"Meaner than snakebite," Clint growled, "what them two done. Might as well cut the legs right out from under a man, as take his truck."

There was more to the story, Gracie knew. How it had rained—a shower, at first, growing to a downpour, and how Uncle Miltie had managed to fashion protective cover for Clint.

It had been impossible to start a fire, he'd said. Not that they had anything to cook, but at least it would have meant some warmth.

By then, Clint's lips were blue, his teeth chattering, and his eyes nearly closed.

It was at that point that Uncle Miltie had heard the search party. Clint was too far gone to react. At first he thought he was imagining it since the sound of their names was almost lost in the pelting of rain. So, in the beginning, he didn't even answer. But, suddenly, he realized, rescue was at hand.

Thank You, Lord.

And then, the rescue team had stabilized Clint and gotten both men out of the woods and to a hospital.

"That's when I called you, Gracie dear, when we got to their vehicles."

She grimaced.

He made a face in agreement. "That phone! I could have done better just hollering."

"But you did call," she said softly. "You called, and I knew at least that you were alive."

Gracie walked with Rocky to his car. He tapped his notebook.

"He's a genuine hero!" he said. "You must be very proud of him."

Indeed she was.

"Imagine! Not only getting his friend past the heart attack, but half-carrying him all that way back."

"And then lugging along that improvised sled." She said quietly, "He simply could not have done it, not under his own power."

Rocky looked at her. "You mean God, I suppose."

"Yes." She held her breath. How she yearned for Rocky to accept the faith that came to her so naturally! "I do mean God."

He said only, "Makes us somewhat younger folks look like marshmallows."

"You would have done exactly the same!" Gracie said stoutly.

He grinned. "I'm planning when I'm eighty to be just as gutsy as he is." He paused. "But I still won't be able to keep up with you!"

OBVIOUSLY, THERE WAS GOING to be an overflow crowd for the Mason City town council meeting. The parking lot was full, adjoining streets lined bumper to bumper, and it was only after much grumbling exploration that Rocky squeezed his little black car into an improbably tiny space.

It was a night cooled by a soft breeze and enlivened by a mini-concerto of muted small-city sounds.

Gracie had to admit that having Rocky at her side was a good thing. They walked easily in tandem, not talking but drawing strength from the ease of their companionship.

"It's a perfect night," she said quietly.

"Depends."

"Depends?" she challenged. "On what?"

"On how you plan to spend it." When she didn't respond, he suggested, "A perfect night for rowing down a gentle river with your best girl across from you."

"What a romantic! There'd be mosquitoes—"

"Not with this breeze!"

She caught his arm. "A perfect night for walking through the woods, playing hopscotch with the patches of moonlight."

"Now you have it, dear girl! Or, a perfect night for digging earthworms for a day's fishing."

She thought of something that seemed to her even worse. "A perfect night for shopping at the mall?"

He groaned. "But what it's not is a perfect night for a shouting match in Mason City, which is what we're about to witness. That much I know."

And yet, as they entered the large room, everything seemed calm.

The very quietness suggested a storm about to break. Around the room the factions were loosely grouped: the stadium supporters in their ancient, ill-fitting letter jackets; the environmentalists looking like earnest academics and '60s refugees, and the businessmen, of course, in jackets and ties.

Picket signs rested against the wall at the rear of the room, and Gracie suspected that Gillian had plans for them before the evening was over.

It might be a very long meeting. At the very least it would try the patience of the panel of council members sitting at the long, blue-draped table on the low platform. While they chatted and shuffled papers, Gracie recognized an underlying tension among them, as well.

She felt a surge of sympathy. When Elmo had been mayor

of Willow Bend, all those years ago, she had often sensed a similar mood when opposing sides turned up to present their positions. Friendships often went out the window and some grudges were never relinquished.

Even though she had come late into the Mason City controversy, she felt invested in it. It truly mattered that Dogwood Park might be sacrificed to the spread of commerce. Yet she also was able to identify with the former athletes. She certainly would feel threatened if a super highway were rerouted through the familiar kitchen of her house, where she, too, had experienced "triumphs."

A gavel banged the meeting to order. A few announcements boomed through a static-impaired sound system.

Lord, show us some solution that will allow all here to leave feeling they have achieved their goals.

Someone stood and cleared his throat. "We want to thank all of you public-spirited citizens who have come together tonight."

A low rumble of voices rose and fell in response.

"Therefore, it seems appropriate that we discharge the business which interests you before getting on to more mundane matters." He looked out. "Who is speaking first?"

Tyrone Sanders took the stage. Surveying the crowd, he paused dramatically before finally beginning. "I'd like to say only a few words now, then reserve the right to speak when the other sides have been presented. There are some 'givens' here: that the area needs more jobs, that we must entice more visitors to the city, that the Brookerman Mall people have made us a most attractive offer. But it's an offer that stands only if they can build on the site they have chosen—" He lifted a page on a flip-chart and pointed. "Here—"

"Save our stadium! Save our stadium! Save our stadium!"

"—or here."

"Save Dogwood Park for the children!"

"Stadium!"

"Park!"

"*Stadium!*"

"*Park!*"

Sanders raised a placating hand, which merely served to intensify the outcry. A gavel banged. It was only when the council president threatened a close to the meeting that the jeers and hoots subsided to a quiet mutter.

"Brookerman has offered—as a bonus on final signing—to build a new stadium, a state-of-the-art facility ..."

The mutter swelled upward, again filling the room.

The gavel banged again.

Sanders made a gesture of frustration. "What is it you people want!"

What a silly question, Gracie thought. They want to keep their stadium. How much clearer can they be?

Next, a spokesman for the former Mason City athletes presented their plea. A new stadium was needed. They recognized that. But the memories attached to the old one made it too precious for demolition. The alumni had pledged a large sum of money to restore the old stadium, both as a memorial and museum.

"Save our park! Save our park!"

Gillian now quieted her followers. Then, one by one and silently, they accepted placards and arranged themselves across the front of the room, with their backs to the platform, leaving space in the center for Deke and Professor Plunkett. When Gillian beckoned, Gracie joined them.

Darius Plunkett was pulling a luggage cart loaded with three large, flat cardboard boxes. While he extracted poster-sized paintings of buildings and arranged them along the front of the stage, Deke replaced the flip chart Tyrone Sanders had been using with his own.

From her position facing the audience, Gracie was able to see little of what was taking place on the stage. However, she could sense Rocky's heightened attention from his furious note-taking. Suddenly, Gillian led her followers off to the side of the room, from which angle they could view the Plunkett/Brandt presentation.

And what they saw was amazing! Most of the building replicas were recognizable, but each had received a "facelift" comparable to that on Deke's putative stained glass shop. Second-floor windows were fitted with shutters, and a variety of businesses occupied the ground floor suites.

Where chimneys had been dilapidated, now they were shown straightened, and all window frames repaired and repainted. The effect was charming but also human. It was a street anyone would want to live on or visit, Gracie thought.

Deke took the microphone. "We'd like to share our vision of what the new shopping center *could* look like. This plan calls for destroying neither our stadium nor our park. Rather it's about giving new life to a section of Mason City that has seemed all but forgotten."

He flipped a sheet and pointed to a map of the blighted neighborhood. "All these buildings require is respect, plus some imagination and repair. Residents of this part of our city have a high unemployment rate and—until now—have had little encouragement to improve their surroundings."

Professor Plunkett went on to explain how in many other towns determined citizens' groups had created unique shopping centers by concentrating on crafts and other artisanal products.

"Goods not found in your ordinary mall stores. As a result, when news of this difference spreads and attracts interest, we might hope tourists will begin to turn up. And, perhaps most important, we retain control locally, rather than placing ourselves at the mercy of developers from who knows where."

During the presentation, Gracie noticed members of the council whispering among themselves and looking thoughtful. More than one head had been nodding.

Members of the audience leaned forward, seeming fascinated. No one muttered or fidgeted now. And Tyrone Sanders? Gracie took a moment to seek him out. He stood off to one side, fingertips idly tapping. Had he already cut some sweet deal with the developers? If he felt that his stake was at risk, he hid it well. Maybe he even liked what he saw?

"Any questions?" Deke asked. He and the professor dealt with each one sensibly and sincerely until the audience held no more raised hands.

At length, Tyrone Sanders signaled that he had a question. "What if the developers find this an attractive alternative—do you see a possible role for them?"

Deke looked to Darius Plunkett, who flipped a page, and with deft strokes sketched a possible arrangement of new buildings. "This might be one solution."

He tore off the page and began another. "Or—if they'd prefer . . . there's some flexibility here. . . ."

Amazing! Gracie thought. His lines were as rapid and certain as if the marker were part of his hand, a sixth finger with a facility for turning concepts into recognizable images.

And suddenly she knew: Darius Plunkett was the phantom artist!

He had to be.

Deke Brandt had never really fit the profile, but the man known as Professor Plunkett possessed both the confidence and the playfulness to enjoy being a prankster. His wit would inspire him to paint the patriotic stars on the rump of a Civil War general's steed, while his human decency and love of beauty inspired the decoration of the stepping stones and the splendid improvements at the playground. How he had hauled all that equipment around, Gracie couldn't help but wonder. She looked at the man with a fresh rush of respect. He and Deke had now finished, and the crowd responded with applause, to which Gracie added her own.

It's going to happen, isn't it, Lord?

Excitement coursed through her. Gillian was on her way to her goal—and so was Professor Plunkett. Together they could transform the world, or at least their particular corner, if they set their minds to it.

Smiling, she watched them.

Only one jarring note marred her pleasure. Whatever could have possessed him to play that unkind practical joke at the beauty parlor? And who had been making those mocking phone calls to Gillian? Who threw the concrete that destroyed Deke's window?

More than one person, obviously, was making mischief in the environs of Mason City.

There was simply no way it could have been Darius Plunkett. Of this she was certain.

I JUST WON'T BE ABLE TO REST," Gracie declared, "until I find out about that hair color mess. There has to be an explanation and, as far as we know, it's never happened again."

She and Marge sat in Gracie's kitchen, sipping tea and enjoying still-warm gingersnaps. Outside in the garden, just beyond range of the inviting aroma of baking apple crisp, Clint Whitley dozed, a hunting and fishing magazine lying open in his lap. Uncle Miltie and Gooseberry lounged in the hammock, much to Charlotte's dismay. The spunky little Shih-Tzu had given up her attempts to inveigle Gooseberry into play and was openly sulking.

"Poor Charlotte." Marge sighed, watching her. "I've often felt the same way."

"What way is that?" Gracie asked, though she had seen her friend in a similar mood many times before.

"Abandoned. Lonely. Unappreciated."

"Marge Lawrence!" chided Grace. "You are definitely not unappreciated! Not by the customers who depend on your shop for its eclectic mix of goodies. Not by me, certainly!"

"Oh, Gracie, it's not the same thing and you know it. Don't *you* ever feel alone? Deserted?"

Gracie thought over memories still too fresh for frequent revival. Yes, of course, she often felt lonely. For example, she missed El across from her at mealtime, praising her cooking—even during those early months of marriage, when the biscuits were overbaked and the meat undercooked. She was lonely for his head on the adjoining pillow, so close that she could feel his steady breath.

Even though she knew the accident that had killed him had been just that—an accident—she had felt abandoned, and a bit angry at El, and at God, too. Her anger had lasted beyond the funeral home, the cemetery, and during weeks—and months—of healing.

Marge was waiting for her answer.

Gracie said simply, "Of course. Everyone does sometimes."

Marge gave a smug nod. "Now—about the beauty shop fiasco—it certainly is a puzzler." She reached for another gingersnap, drew her hand back, and then gave in to temptation.

"And knowing you, Gracie Lynn Parks, we'll need to make a run to Mason City and do some sleuthing." She leaned forward. "While we're there, aren't you curious to see how the development's coming along?"

Gracie rose with resolve. "As soon as the oven timer goes off, we're leaving."

"Well . . . I suppose it *could* wait until we try out the apple crisp. Do you have any French vanilla ice cream?"

Harriet's Hair Salon was enjoying a leisurely day. Only three stylists were in evidence as Marge and Gracie entered. It was difficult to equate the sleepy scene with the frenzied events of Gracie's earlier visit. Even the sharp chemical aromas seemed muted.

Only the proprietress was animated. "Ladies," she greeted them. "What can I do for you today?"

"We don't have an appointment—" Gracie began.

"No problem. When it's this slow, we take walk-ins." She raised an eyebrow. "Looks like you could use a touch-up, dear."

Gracie nodded. "I . . . well, I nearly had one here a few weeks ago."

"Oh? And someone refused to take you? Do you remember which—"

Gracie laughed. "It was just that the color effects that day were . . . unusual."

"Oh!" Harriet Langhorne lost her composure, then quickly regained it. "Believe it or not, that prank turned out to be not an entirely bad thing. Did you happen to see the blue job?"

"She liked it!" Gracie remembered. "The other three customers were distraught, but she seemed afraid you'd force her to change hers."

Leading Gracie and Marge to a cushioned wicker love seat and taking the matching chair opposite, Harriet confided, "Would you believe, dear, that she still loves it? Comes back now to have it redyed in a color that won't wash out."

She leaned forward, saying in a confidential tone, "And even more amazing, there are now three other customers who've asked for blue! Isn't that extraordinary?"

She stood. "Now, about that touch-up—"

"Only if you'll answer a question for me. For us." Gracie reached to draw Marge into the discussion.

"Happy to!"

Marge gushed, "We're consumed with curiosity! Who 'done' it?"

"My daughter Glynnis! It was to get back at her father and me. She was dating this young man we didn't much like, and we'd forbidden her to see him for at least six weeks. In which time, I'll admit, we'd hoped to brainwash her."

She sighed. "She's still seeing him, but we've gotten to know him better, and . . ." Her voice drifted off. "Anyway, she's one of the manicurists."

Gracie remembered. "The one you asked to help with rinses. I remember."

"When we asked whatever had made her think of such a diabolical thing—"

Gracie guessed, "The statue in the park."

"Thank goodness she had sense enough not to use permanent dye! Here, dear, let's take you at this chair over here. I'll do you myself! That's a very becoming shade of red!"

Perched high on a paint-spattered ladder, Darius Plunkett used a slender brush on the scroll shape of an Ionic half-column. "This will be a gift shop," he said. "You know, cards and things."

"Marge has one like that." Gracie added, "Marge Lawrence, Darius Plunkett."

He suspended his brushing, leaned down, and left a dab of moss-green paint on Marge's palm. "Happy to meet you."

Closing her fingers over the paint smear, Marge drew a deep breath. "And you," she said, her admiring voice huskier than usual.

Gracie hid a grin. Marge was easily smitten. She'd get over it. But she might not wash that hand for a few weeks.

Darius Plunkett turned to the second pillar. Suddenly a black cat streaked beneath the ladder, a determined mutt in hot pursuit. The professor kept his balance with some difficulty.

"Never fear, ladies." He applied a few more delicate strokes. "I once was part of a troop of acrobats, so this is mere child's play."

Actor. Artist. Teacher. A published author. Acrobat. What had the man *not* done?

Gracie asked, "Are the developers coming around?"

"You bet! The only problem is keeping them reined in! They'd take over the whole complex, if we allowed them to."

"Congratulations are in order."

He shrugged. "Maybe."

"But everyone's happy now, right?"

He said dryly, "Human nature being what it is, that's highly unlikely."

Gracie waited. He placed a few more brush strokes before resuming.

"But, well, yes, to answer your question honestly, most people are content now. And Gillian?" His voice softened. "Well, Gillian's in her element. Leaders need followers, and Gillian Pomeroy can lead me, for one, anywhere she chooses."

He asked Gracie contritely, "Will you forgive me for pretending to be such a hard-luck case when we first met?"

"I like this version of you a lot better!" Gracie replied.

Plunkett acknowledged her with a lift of his brush.

"And now that the threatening phone calls are done with—"

"Oh?" Gracie's heart beat a bit faster. "And the broken window?"

He chuckled. "Young hoodlums. When adults act like unruly brats, what more can we expect? Their parents dragged them over by the scruff of their necks to apologize. And make restitution out of their allowances."

Gracie breathed a quick prayer of thanks for parents who cared enough to discipline.

"Personally, I'd have voted for four hours or so on the rack—but Gillian's forgiven them, so I suppose I must, too."

He paused in his painting. "You're leaving already?

"Our work is done here," Marge said, somewhat dramatically.

Plunkett raised an eyebrow. "As in 'Who was that masked man?' Well, if you must leave, cheerio!"

"So long!" they called back.

"Nice to meet you!" Marge added.

Gracie teased, "I think you'll have a better chance with Clint Whitley."

"Don't give me any ideas!" Marge retorted. "I'm sure Uncle Miltie would like to be my maid of honor!"

AMY GREETED THEM with a stack of menus. "Abe says he'll join you, so a table for six it is."

She added courteously, "I suppose you'd rather be away from a window, since it's so gloomy out?"

Pastor Paul said, "We make our own sunshine. Besides, I like to see the flowers growing."

"Looks like mostly dandelions from here," she observed, but she led the way to a window table.

Gallantly holding a chair for Gracie, Pastor Paul said, "Amy, dear child, I consider the dandelion a perfect metaphor for people of faith."

"Because they're pests?" grumbled Rocky.

"Rocky . . . ," warned Gracie.

She smiled an apology toward Pastor Paul. "That's all right," he said, helping Marge and Uncle Miltie get settled before taking his own chair. "I hope we do pester the world, enough to get them thinking about what's truly important. Jesus was certainly considered a pest in his time. Just ask any scribe or Pharisee!"

"Did I hear my name mentioned?" Abe offered his hand to each in turn before taking the sixth chair. "So, brother Paul, what have we of the Jewish persuasion done now?"

Pastor Paul laughed. "You, my friend, are no Pharisee! On the contrary, you are the most ecumenical of men!"

"And yet, who knows, in another time or place...?"

"No matter when," Amy told him, "your kindness would have made you who you are, the same as you are."

Abe grinned fondly. "Is that logical? I think it's my favorite waitress's heart speaking. But I don't know that she's not right. I probably am an old softie today and would have been two thousand years ago!"

He looked at Amy and winked. She winked back.

"She grows more beautiful every day, don't you think, Gracie?"

"Puts us all in the shade," confirmed Uncle Miltie. "By the way, do you know what a seal and a cedar tree have in common?"

"He's b-a-a-ack!" Rocky observed dryly.

Marge groaned. "Wouldn't it make sense to order first?"

Amy dimpled. "How long will this joke take, Mr. Morgan?"

"Begone, lass," he growled. But Marge protested, "Not before we order!"

"Now," Abe said, when Amy had gone to the kitchen, "we

must establish an agenda. I myself want to learn more about these Pharasaic dandelions. We are all also panting to hear what seals and cedar trees—is that right—have in common?" He added, "And Gracie must tell us what the redheaded woodpecker has decided for her life."

Marge frowned.

"A story," Rocky explained. "One of our host's legendary moral tales with the ending still unresolved."

"Parables, I believe you would call them. But, perhaps, we should begin with the seals . . . since we don't want a punchline interrupted by something as mundane as food."

Uncle Miltie cleared his throat. "The question was, as you'll remember—"

In unison, they all recited, "What do a seal and a cedar tree have in common?"

"Yes." Uncle Miltie waited. No guesses were forthcoming.

Just then, Amy appeared with their food.

"Our meals are ready!" Uncle Miltie reached for his napkin. "Barks," he said. "Seals and cedars—they both have barks."

Rocky gave a short laugh. "You mean, you've come back to drive us all barking mad!"

Uncle Miltie sniffed haughtily and picked up his fork.

Somehow, somewhere, Uncle Miltie had found a Roy Rogers rerun. Gooseberry napped in Gracie's lap, more interested in his dreams than old cowboy stars. Gently, his mistress stroked his head and watched Uncle Miltie watching Roy Rogers and

Dale Evans make the West safe for everyone but the bad guys.

The problem is, Lord, that we're all bad guys, to some extent. We make the mistake of thinking that our sins aren't all that glaring, comparatively. But we don't see as You do, and—if Shakespeare doesn't mind a paraphrase—a sin by any other name would . . . still be sin.

I really liked what Pastor Paul said today about dandelions. Wonderful how—with Abe there—he didn't just say Christians, but "people of faith." How we need to be omnipresent, like dandelions, and as stubborn as they are, even in the face of persecution. How we must be persistent in spreading the good news, never allowing ourselves to become discouraged.

Thank You for Pastor Paul, for his oh-so-down-to-earth way of presenting Your Gospel. Thank You that today, for a change, Rocky seemed to have listened with an open mind. Thank You for bringing Uncle Miltie and Clint Whitley home safe and sound. Thank You for the marvelous things that are happening in Mason City—and for allowing me to be a small part of them.

Lord, my life is so rich and full! Every day, I think of new blessings, find new proofs of Your love.

Uncle Miltie's head drooped, then jerked awake, but just for a few minutes. Dislodging Gooseberry with great care, and waiting to turn off the television until the last notes of "Happy Trails" had been heard, Gracie headed off to the kitchen, still humming along. She was going to cook some of her Bountiful Soup for dinner.

Until we meet again. . . .

Gracie's Bountiful Soup

- ✓ 1 large onion, finely chopped
- ✓ 1 medium cauliflower, cut into small chunks
- ✓ 4 ounces spinach, pulled into bits
- ✓ 1 large red pepper, chopped
- ✓ 1 large green pepper, chopped
- ✓ 1 large yellow pepper, chopped
- ✓ 6 to 8 celery sticks, chopped
- ✓ 2 to 3 large carrots, thinly sliced
- ✓ 1 to 2 tablespoons of crushed cumin and coriander seed
- ✓ 1 pint chicken broth
- ✓ One 13-ounce can of tomatoes
- ✓ Juice of half of a large lemon or lime
- ✓ 1/2 cup of chopped flat parsley
- ✓ 2 to 3 garlic cloves

Place all of the vegetables (except the tomatoes), along with the crushed cumin and coriander seeds, in a large pot. Add the chicken stock, plus extra water if necessary, to cover. Heat this until it boils, and then add the tomatoes and lemon (or lime) juice. Toss in the fresh flat parsley and the garlic cloves. Simmer until all of the ingredients are tender, which should take around a half-hour.

Gracie says, "I call this my Bountiful Soup because it really is! To make it even heartier, sometimes I include a diced potato or maybe even a handful of elbow macaroni. But even better is to throw in—toward the end of the cooking time—one of those packets of miniature prepared pastas that the Willow Mart stocks in its refrigerated case. Usually I choose the sort stuffed with spinach, cheese and herbs, which adds extra delicious texture to the soup. Garlic bread or Parmesan cheese toasts are the perfect accompaniment."

About the Author

"This is my favorite place on earth," Evelyn says of the three acres (former apple orchard and sheep pasture) where husband Fred built their ranch-style home more than forty years ago. Pennsylvania white-tailed deer, enticed by fallen apples, venture from the lower half-acre, once a pasture for their three daughters' horses, but now a tangle of shrubs and lofty oaks.

Thirteen flowerbeds (so far) interrupt the flow of lawn. Every Sunday, spring through fall, Evelyn takes flowers to church. "It's a tradition going back, at least, to my grandmother," she explains. "Mother continued the ministry in my grandmother's memory. I continue it in Mother's."

Her mother not only nurtured a love of nature but also taught a reverence for words. "My father surrounded us with music and encouraged my art, but I'm a writer because of Mother. And I'm a better writer due to my husband's incredible tolerance for clutter . . . and because our daughters were my best literary critics ever." Valerie, Melanie and Robin also served as puppeteers and technicians for plays sometimes completed on the way to the performance.

"What I am not," Evelyn admits, "is organized." What she is, is an author of twenty-five published books, erstwhile artist, compulsive teacher, gardener, baker-of-cookies, knitter-of-booties she gives away often to strangers and an unapologetically proud grandmother. Granddaughter Micky attends Vanderbilt University. Grandsons Jonathan and Benjamin are in elementary school.

DATE DUE			

07-06

Minshull, Evelyn

Mischief in Mason City